YOU'RE

"I can't believe y... ... ...
exclaimed in the h... ... ...

"Even *I* noticed," Alex said. "And I'm not exactly what you'd call observant."

Carrie glanced down, then rolled her eyes. "I guess that's why you're wearing two different sneakers."

Alex looked surprised, then blushed. "I had a lot on my mind this morning. I just grabbed what was on the floor. Good thing Rachel's not copying *me*. At least Sky's shoes always match."

Sky closed her locker. "Shh, she'll hear you." She darted her eyes to the left where Rachel Harris hovered around the second bank of lockers. Sky bit her lip. Were Carrie and Alex right? Was Rachel Harris watching Sky's every move and mimicking her?

M·a·k·i·n·g F·r·i·e·n·d·s

All *Making Friends* titles can be ordered at your local bookshop or are available by post from Book Service by Post (tel: 01624 675137).

Making Friends

You're fab, Rachel

Kate Andrews

MACMILLAN CHILDREN'S BOOKS

First published 1998 by Macmillan Children's Books
a division of Macmillan Publishers Limited
25 Eccleston Place, London SW1W 9NF
and Basingstoke

Associated companies throughout the world

ISBN 0 330 36934 2

1 3 5 7 9 8 6 4 2

A CIP catalogue record for this book is available from
the British Library

Printed and bound in Great Britain by Mackays of Chatham plc, Kent

The cast of
M·a·k·i·n·g F·r·i·e·n·d·s

Alex

Age: 13

Looks: Light brown hair, blue eyes

Family: Mother died when she was a baby; lives with her dad and her brother Matt, aged 14

Likes: Skateboarding; her family and friends; wearing baggy T-shirts and jeans; being adventurous; letting her feelings show!

Dislikes: People who make fun of her skateboard, her brother or her dad; dressing smart or girly; anything to do with maths or science; dishonesty

Carrie

Age: 13

Looks: Long dark hair – often dyed black! Hazel eyes

Family: Awful! No brothers or sisters; very rich parents who go on about money all the time

Likes: Writing stories; wearing black (drives her mum mad!); thinking deep thoughts; Sky's parents and their awesome houseboat!

Dislikes: Her full name – Carrington; her parents; her mum's choice of clothes; jokes about her hair; computers

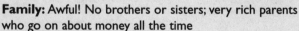

Sky

Age: 13

Looks: Light brown skin, dark hair, brown eyes

Family: Crazy! Lives on a houseboat with weird parents and a brother, Leif, aged 8

Likes: Shopping; trendy gear; TV; pop music; talking!

Dislikes: Her parents' bizarre lifestyle; having no money; eating meat

Jordan

Age: 13

Looks: Floppy fair hair, green eyes

Family: Uncomfortable! Four big brothers – all so brilliant at sports he can never compete with them

Likes: Drawing! (especially cartoons); basketball (but don't tell anyone!); playing sax (badly); taking the mickey out of his brothers

Dislikes: Being "baby brother" to four brainless apes; Sky when she starts gossiping

Sam

Age: 13

Looks: Native-American; very dark hair, very dark eyes

Family: Confusing! Both parents are Native-American but have different views on how their kids should look and behave; one sister – Shawna, aged 16

Likes: Skateboarding with Alex; computers (especially surfing the Net); writing for the school paper; goofing around

Dislikes: The way his friends dump their problems on each other; his parents' arguments

Amy

Age: 13

Looks: Sickeningly gorgeous blonde hair; baby blue eyes (yuck!)

Family: Spoilt rotten by her dad, which worries her mum; two big sisters

Likes: Having loads of expensive clothes; making other people feel stupid; Matt (Alex's brother) – she fancies him; being leader of "The Amys" – her bunch of snobby friends

Dislikes: Alex, Carrie and Sky! Looking stupid or childish

Mel

Age: 13

Looks: Black hair, dark eyes

Family: Nice parents who work very hard to do their best for Mel

Likes: Her mum and dad; her friends – but should these be the Amys, or Alex, Carrie and Sky? Standing up for herself; reading horror novels

Dislikes: Amy, when she's rotten to other people; worrying about who are her **real** friends

Rachel

Age: 13

Looks: Long, straight, brown hair, hazel eyes. Wears glasses until Sky makes her over and her mum agrees to pay for contacts

Family: Hard work! Single mum works long hours as a nurse to support the family, so Rachel ends up spending lots of time looking after her kid sister Erin, aged 10

Likes: Movies; Monty Python; science – she wants to be a doctor some day

Dislikes: People who call her a nerd because she's quiet and likes school; egomaniacs and snobs (mentioning no names)

One

"A tuxedo!" The noise above Jordan Sullivan's head was so loud, he had to shout.

His four older brothers were upstairs over the kitchen, goofing around and wrestling—like they did every morning—and it was driving Jordan nuts. It was like trying to eat breakfast under a bowling alley.

He wished they would stop it long enough for him to eat cereal in peace. If they could stop being his brothers, that would be cool, too. Unfortunately they were related to him by birth, and there was nothing he or any of them could do about it.

Luckily all four were in high school. That meant their bus arrived about ten minutes later than Jordan's, so Jordan had ten whole minutes to himself in the

1

morning before they came down for their own breakfast.

A loud *kaboom* echoed over his head. Mrs. Sullivan's eyes rolled upward and studied the ceiling. When she seemed confident it wasn't about to fall in, she turned her attention back to Jordan. "A tuxedo!" she confirmed.

"You've got to be kidding!" The thought of himself in a tuxedo complete with cummerbund made Jordan laugh so hard, he sucked a cornflake down his windpipe and began to choke.

"I'm not kidding." Jordan's mother came around the corner of the kitchen counter with a glass of water.

Jordan took a grateful sip and composed himself. "Sorry. It's just that, well, I'm not really the Ken doll type."

Mrs. Sullivan laughed and returned to her morning battle station behind the kitchen counter. She was petite, blond, and had blue eyes that could look as sweet as an angel's eyes or hard as rocks.

When he got home from school, Jordan could always tell whether or not his brothers had gotten into trouble just by looking at his mother's eyes.

If they were hard and bright blue, he knew to keep his head low.

He watched his mother as she prepared the boys' lunches. She quickly spread mayo on thirty-six slices of bread and wiped the excess on a dish towel stuck in the belt of her jeans. Then she stuck the knife in the mustard and repeated the process. Food was serious business around the Sullivan household. "Three sandwiches or four?" she asked Jordan, slapping meat and cheese on the bread slices.

"Mom!" Jordan squeaked. "I'm not the Arnold Schwarzenegger type, either. *One* sandwich, two max, would be plenty. But I buy my lunch, anyway, remember?"

Jordan's brothers always brought bagged lunches. They said the portions in the high school cafeteria were too small.

His mother didn't seem to be listening. She had once more turned her attention to the ceiling. Round two had started. Jordan heard a series of thumps and yells. The light fixture over the kitchen table swayed back and forth.

Jordan grimaced. "You're overfeeding them. No wonder they're so out of control. If you don't believe me, ask any veterinarian that specializes in large animals."

Jordan's brothers were huge by any mammalian standards. All four of them were star basketball players. And all four of them ate, like, fifteen times their weight every twenty-four hours. It was just *amazing* how much they could put away. Jordan couldn't figure out how his parents could afford to keep them alive.

It was a good thing they were afraid of their mother. Without her to protect him, Jordan sometimes wondered if they might not just slap *him* between a couple of slices of whole wheat and gobble him up. They were always threatening to. It wasn't easy being the runt in a litter of five.

Jordan cheered himself up at night by imagining his father announcing to the Four Stooges that they were just too darned expensive, so he was putting them up for adoption. Better yet—renting them out to the local garbage hauler.

Sure, it was pure wishful thinking, but a guy could dream, couldn't he? Jordan was definitely a dreamer. One look at his imaginative cartoons proved that.

But finding a quiet spot to dream and draw in this house was practically a mission impossible. Jordan's brothers were way rowdy. Not to mention obnoxious. Their favorite sport after basketball was competitive Jordan torture.

Upstairs, something really big fell on the floor. Something even bigger fell on top of it. A light sprinkling of plaster rained down on the kitchen table.

"That does it!" Mrs. Sullivan put down the knife, reached for the broom, and knocked on the ceiling. "Hey!" Her sharp warning bark was so loud, Jordan jumped. Hard to believe that such a small, pretty woman could produce a sound like a police officer. Jordan figured she'd had to learn to bark like that in self-defense. He knew that being a mother to four gorillas and one incredibly witty monkey couldn't be easy.

Her shout was loud enough to be heard upstairs because the noise above them stopped.

Jordan sighed. His brothers were *such* a pain in the neck. Someday, he thought happily, he would grow up and live in a house with adjustable ceilings. That way if any of his brothers threatened to visit, he could make the ceilings really low. And if they still *did* visit, *they'd* get a pain in the neck.

After closing down the destruction derby upstairs, Mrs. Sullivan looked across the kitchen counter at Jordan. "How many sandwiches did you say?"

He waved his arms. "None. It's me. Jordan. The frail, weedy, *sensitive* child. Remember?"

Jordan's silliness got a smile out of his mom. "You're not frail, and you're not weedy. But you *are* sensitive—thank goodness—which is why I know I can count on you to understand how important this occasion is."

Jordan groaned. Arguing with his mom was like debating with a heat-seeking missile. There was no escape. You could run, but you couldn't hide. No matter how smoothly he changed the subject, she always managed to lead the conversation back to the target. He sighed. If his mother wanted him to wear a tux to his cousin

Margaret's sweet sixteen party, resistance was futile.

Jordan poured himself some more cereal and watched his mother bag the lunches. "Okay, okay. I'm in. I'll wear a tux."

"And?" she prompted.

"I'll . . . I'll . . ." He gulped, hesitating to say it out loud. Once he said it out loud, it was a done deal. He wouldn't be able to back out.

"You'll bring a girl," his mother finished for him.

"Do I have to?" Jordan asked feebly. "It's not like *I'm* sixteen. I'm only fourteen. I'm in the eighth grade. I'm way too young to date," he declared solemnly.

"Don't be silly. Nobody's talking about your bringing a *date*. Just bring a friend. A friend who's a girl. Jordan, your cousin Margaret's sweet sixteen party is going to be the biggest and most formal event this family has held since your aunt Carla's last wedding—"

"Would that be the tenth husband or the eleventh?" Jordan asked wryly.

"The fourth," his mother said. "Don't be

smart. All I want is for my sons to suit up, show up, and bring somebody to dance with."

Jordan groaned.

"Why is this such a problem?" she asked, lifting her shoulders in bewilderment. "You're not afraid of girls. You have some darling female friends."

"I have three. That's the problem," Jordan said. "Which one should I invite?"

"That's entirely up to you," Mrs. Sullivan replied.

"Thanks. That's a big help."

Outside, a horn honked. Jordan looked at the kitchen clock. "There's the bus. Gotta go." Jordan shoved the last bite of cereal in his mouth and jumped up. He kissed his mother on the cheek. "Bye."

"Invite someone today," Mrs. Sullivan urged as he ran through the living room and into the front hall.

Just as he was opening the door, the four doofuses came thundering down the stairs for their own morning meal.

"Hey, runt!" Doofus Number 1 grunted.

"Comin' through!" Doofus Number 2 yelled.

"Heads up!" Doofus Number 3 hooted.

Doofus Number 4 made a boarlike snorting sound and lifted his hand. Jordan ducked out the door before the huge paw could clobber him.

Outside, the morning was cool and crisp. Jordan broke into a run and took the bus steps two at a time.

"Whoaa!" Brick, the driver of bus number four, reared back in mock surprise. "Running from the bro pack?"

Jordan laughed. Brick had been driving the school bus for a few years now. He'd known Jordan's brothers when they were in middle school. He also knew that Jordan played pranks on them, which meant that periodically Jordan was either on the run or in hiding.

"A narrow escape today." Jordan grinned and hurried toward the back of the bus. For once he wished that he and his four best friends didn't *always* sit together in the back. This morning he really wanted to talk to Sam one-on-one. Man-to-man. That was hard to do with Carrie Mersel, Skyler Foley, and Alexandra "Alex" Wagner sitting right there.

"Hey, loser," Carrie said as he slipped into the seat next to Alex. Carrie and Jordan were good buddies, but they enjoyed trading friendly insults.

"Good morning, sunshine," he said. Calling Carrie anything associated with brightness was more insulting to her than any standard school yard slam.

Sky and Alex giggled. Sam rolled his eyes. "Lame," he pronounced.

"I don't think so," Sky said with a mischievous smile. "Carrie is just full of sunshine this morning."

"Yeah, right," Carrie grumbled.

"She told Brick if he didn't slow down over the speed humps, she was going to barf—*on him*," Alex said.

Jordan laughed. Carrie's sarcastic sense of humor was the coolest thing about her. "Why the evil 'tude?" he asked. "Did your mom threaten to dress you up in pink lace?"

"No," Carrie said. "But she did start in on the computer thing again this morning."

"Ohhhhh," Jordan said. Carrie and her mother had an ongoing argument about computers versus typewriters. Mrs. Mersel

10

was totally into the wonderful world of modern technology. Carrie hated computers and anything related to them. She wrote all her gruesome horror stories on an old IBM typewriter.

Suddenly Alex groaned.

"What's the matter?" Jordan asked.

"English test today," she muttered.

"Here, have some gum and cheer up," Sky said, offering a stick to Carrie and then everybody else. "Last chance to chew before school."

"Thanks," Jordan said with a smile. Leave it to *genuinely* sunny Sky to see a simple piece of gum as a pick-me-up.

Carrie popped hers in her mouth and chewed vigorously. "I can already feel my karma improving."

"Yeah," Alex said. "Me too. Gum must have some kind of calmifying effect." She adjusted her Supersonics cap and tucked her skateboard more securely under the seat.

Jordan chewed harder. He didn't feel too calm right now. As he looked at each one of his female friends, he felt nervous and completely clueless about what to do.

He had a feeling that if he chose one of them to take to the party, the other two would be less than happy with him.

His mom was right. Jordan knew three really nice girls he could ask to his cousin's sweet sixteen party.

It would be a whole lot easier if he only knew one.

Two

"I can't believe you haven't noticed," Carrie exclaimed in the hallway after lunch.

"Even *I* noticed," Alex said. "And I'm not exactly what you'd call observant."

Carrie glanced down, then rolled her eyes. "I guess that's why you're wearing two different sneakers."

Alex looked surprised, then blushed. "I had a lot on my mind this morning. I just grabbed what was on the floor. Good thing Rachel's not copying *me*. At least Sky's shoes always match."

Sky closed her locker. "Shhh, she'll hear you." She darted her eyes to the left, where Rachel Harris hovered around the second bank of lockers. Their eyes met briefly. Rachel's cheeks colored. She quickly dropped her gaze and began rustling through her locker.

Sky bit her lip. Were Carrie and Alex

right? Was Rachel Harris watching Sky's every move and mimicking her?

"Rachel looks at you like you're some kind of movie star," Carrie said. "I keep waiting for her to ask you for an autograph."

"Yeah, right." Sky shook her head. She hadn't noticed. In fact, she had never paid any attention at all to Rachel Harris. Nobody did. Rachel was the quietest girl in school. She never had anything to say. And as far as anybody knew, she didn't have any friends.

"I can't believe she has the nerve to wear her hair like that," Carrie whispered.

Rachel had looped braids pinned on top of her head. Sky had worn her hair like that yesterday. No other girl at Robert Lowell had worn that hairstyle. And as a matter of fact, Amy Anderson (Robert Lowell's Number-One School Snot) had teased Sky about it. Sky hadn't paid any attention, though. She knew it was just envy talking.

"Aren't you peeved that Rachel is ripping off your individuality?" Carrie pressed.

Sky knew she had a reputation for being creatively stylish and individual. Actually she *had* to be creative in order to be stylish. Sky's folks didn't have much money, so Sky had learned to put together great looks for next to nothing.

"It wouldn't be so bizarre if Rachel was copying, say, a model," Carrie continued. "Or some cool actress. It would be dumb, but I could understand it. But what kind of person copies somebody in her own grade?"

Sky shrugged. "Okay. It's a little weird, but so what? It's harmless. And it's not like anybody's going to get the two of us confused. So let's not be mean about it, okay? We're starting to sound like The Amys."

Alex lifted her Supersonics cap and scratched her forehead under the bill. "Wouldn't want that."

Carrie pushed her dyed black hair off her shoulders. "Personally, I think a person's individuality is sacred. And I'm not so sure Rachel is harmless, either. She's acting like a stalker or something."

Sky laughed. "Would you get a grip?"

Before Carrie could answer, the bell rang.

"Ugh! I'm dead!" Alex groaned, shouldering her pack and shooting her friends a pathetic look before loping off toward English.

"Good luck on the test!" Sky fluttered her fingers—enjoying the rainbow effect. Last night she had painted each one of her nails a different color.

Carrie and Sky both had the same history class. They started down the hall. "Be careful," Carrie whispered. "She's following you. She's getting closer. She's reaching for her ax. She's . . ."

Sky laughed. "Would you stop?" She turned and saw Rachel walking behind them, hugging her books against her chest.

Carrie was a horror and mystery junkie. She was also a horror and mystery *writer*. Her imagination was hyperactive, and she saw something sinister everywhere she looked.

"Rachel is in our history class," Sky reminded Carrie. "It's pretty logical that she would be walking behind us."

Carrie pressed her lips together. "We'll

see. Watch this. *Oops!*" Carrie pretended to stumble. Her books tumbled out of her arms to the floor. Students veered around Carrie and Sky as they bent to clean up the mess. "If she passes us, she's not following you," Carrie whispered. "If she doesn't pass us, you're being stalked."

Sky was sure that she would see Rachel's feet pass her and Carrie as Rachel hurried to history class.

Sky fumbled with the books and waited. Ten . . . nine . . . eight . . . seven . . . six . . . *So pass us already*, Sky mentally urged. Five . . . four . . . three . . . two . . .

Sky managed to bend her head far enough down to peer between her bent legs. Several yards behind her she saw Rachel's feet—standing still.

Sky stood up quickly and looked back over her shoulder. Rachel immediately pretended to examine a notice pasted on the wall.

Carrie raised an eyebrow at Sky.

Sky decided to take the bull by the horns and just see what would happen. She turned around. "Come on!" she said.

Rachel jumped, and her cheeks turned scarlet.

17

"Come on," Sky repeated with a smile. "We'll be late for class."

Rachel's mouth opened and closed a couple of times. She looked behind her quickly, then back at Sky. "Are you, uh, talking to me?"

"Yeah. You're in our history class, aren't you? You know how Ms. Farley is about being on time."

Rachel's face turned even redder. "Yeah. She's really . . . you know . . . ummm . . . kind of . . . strict," Rachel mumbled. She quickened her steps to catch up with Sky and Carrie but was too shy to look either of them in the eye as she passed them and entered the classroom.

"Told you so," Carrie whispered as she and Sky walked in.

Sky couldn't think of anything to say that didn't sound obnoxious, so she just went to her desk. Rachel took her seat several desks back.

Sky twirled the end of one of her braids. So Carrie and Alex were right. Rachel Harris was following her and copying her every move.

Was it harmless? Sky was going to have to think about that.

Three

"So that's the whole deal," Jordan finished. "What do you think?"

Sam raked his fingers through his short spiky hair. "I think you have a big problem."

Jordan's shoulders slumped. "I was afraid you were going to say that." The two boys were on their way to the tuxedo rental shop after school.

Luckily for Jordan, Sam was free this afternoon. Jordan didn't feel qualified to make a major clothing rental decision with no peer consultation. He also needed some input on how to handle the "bring a girl" thing.

"You don't have *a* problem. You have *two* problems," Sam added, kicking a rock with his foot as they walked along the old-fashioned brick sidewalk. "'Cause no matter who you ask, the other two are going to feel dissed big-time."

"Isn't there some way to ask one without the other two getting bent?" Jordan heard a hint of desperation creep into his voice.

"Nope," Sam said simply.

"Are you sure?"

"I have a sister. I know these things."

"Well, what am I going to do!" Jordan cried, throwing up his arms in frustration.

Sam held up his hands. "Treat this just like any other emergency. Don't panic, and stay calm."

"I can't believe teachers waste our time with fire drills and never give us any useful emergency training—like what to do when you have to ask a girl to a party and no matter who you ask, you're toast."

He stopped. "Hold it. Why don't I pass the buck? Ask Alex, Carrie, and Sky what they think? Let them decide who goes."

Sam shook his head. "They'd each have a different opinion about who should go. Before it was all over, they'd be mad at each other *and* you!"

Jordan sighed. Sam was right. Alex, Sky, and Carrie were as different as three girls could be. It was really unusual for all three to agree on anything. Sometimes Jordan

20

wondered how a tomboy, a mall rat, and a goth girl could be so close.

"Look, you haven't said who *you* would like to invite," Sam pointed out. "If you didn't have this problem with the other two, which one would you ask?"

"Tough call," Jordan answered. "Sky's real friendly and would have no trouble talking to people and all that stuff. But Carrie would definitely have hilarious commentary on my family. And even though Alex is a girl, I feel totally comfortable with her all the time. Being with Alex is like being with a guy."

"I'm not sure she would consider that a compliment," Sam commented.

Jordan started to feel panicked again. "See? I didn't know that. I just don't know anything *about* girls. I'm going to get myself into trouble no matter what I do or say."

Sam gave Jordan a sympathetic look.

"I wish I could invite all three," Jordan muttered, tearing a leaf from a tree and ripping it into little pieces as they walked. "That would solve the problem, and it'd be fun, too."

"Well, you can't," Sam said. "So let's go

do the tux thing and worry about the girl thing later."

They had arrived at Tuxedo Tales, in Ocean View's Old Town Square. Sam pushed open the door, and Jordan followed him into the air-conditioned shop. Jordan looked at the rows of black suits hanging on one wall.

"Gag," Jordan whispered, looking at the clothes.

"Gag and hurl!" Sam whispered back.

Plastic mannequins around the room modeled the very latest in tuxedo styles.

"Unbelievable!" Jordan went over to a lime green tuxedo with a matching bow tie. He gave an exaggerated swallow, pretending he was sick to his stomach.

"That's nothing," Sam said with a snicker. "Look at this!" He held up a novelty cummerbund covered with little Scottie dogs.

Jordan went over to a rack of traditional tuxedos made of shiny polyester. "I don't know much about clothes, but I know a lot about movies. Something tells me this merchandise is not up to James Bond specs." He fingered the lapel of a jacket and wrinkled his nose. "Maybe it's the material.

This feels like it's made out of shredded plastic bottles and recycled disposable diapers."

Sam felt it and then wiped his fingers on his shirt. "James Bond looks totally cool. How does he do it in a dorky outfit like that?"

A salesman was coming toward them from the back of the store.

"Check this guy out," Jordan hissed.

Sam barely stifled a laugh. The guy had on a yellow dinner jacket with a white carnation and white shoes. "May I help you?"

Not in a million years! Jordan took Sam's arm and began backing up. "Uhhh . . . no thanks. We were just looking."

The salesman smirked and turned away.

"Would you watch it!" Sam yelped when Jordan yanked him through the door and out of the shop.

"Sorry. I was afraid I'd crumble under high-pressure salesmanship. Yellow's not a good color on me."

"You promised your mom—"

"I promised her I would wear a tux. I

23

didn't say I'd get one from Tuxedo Tales."
Jordan bounced thoughtfully on the toes of
his athletic shoes. "I want a tuxedo with
some style. I want a tuxedo with some
history. I want a tuxedo that's *lived!*"

Sam grinned. "Vintage, right?"

Jordan cocked his finger like a gun and
pointed it at Sam. "You got it," he said,
trying to talk with a British accent like
James Bond. "What do you say we check
out the Vintage Voice?"

Sam smiled. "Cool. Maybe I can find
that leather jacket I've been looking for."

Jordan took some deep breaths. Just
talking like James Bond was making him
feel more in control of the situation. Cocky,
even.

"You know what I think I'm going to
do?" Jordan continued in his James Bond
voice. "I'm going to put their names in a
hat and pick one. Then I'll let the winner
tell the other two all about her incredible
luck."

Sam elbowed him. "Trouble at twelve
o'clock, *Mr. Bond!*"

Jordan looked to see what Sam was
talking about and did a double take. "Oh

no!" He felt beads of sweat pop out along his hairline.

Carrie, Alex, and Sky had just come out of the pharmacy and were walking straight toward Jordan and Sam. At least Carrie and Sky were walking. Alex was rolling slowly along on her skateboard—backward.

All Jordan's cocky confidence evaporated. He felt a hot, guilty flush spread over his cheeks and neck. "Get away from that door," Jordan hissed at Sam. "They might get suspicious."

Sam jumped away from the doorway of Tuxedo Tales as if the pavement had turned into a hot plate. The two boys turned so that they no longer faced the window and took several steps away.

The girls spotted them and waved. Alex expertly pivoted on her board and came skidding over. "What are you doing here?" She popped the skateboard into the air with the thick toe of her sneaker and caught it. Carrie and Sky closed in.

Jordan swallowed. "We were . . . uh . . . uh . . ." Jordan's heart hammered. "What are we doing here, Sam?"

"We were looking for you guys," Sam improvised—brilliantly in Jordan's opinion.

"We had a feeling you guys went to the pharmacy, so we decided to walk over and see if we were right," Jordan added.

Sky took a bite of her granola bar. "Why?"

"Why?" Jordan repeated blankly.

Sky held out the bar to Jordan and Sam. "Yeah. Why?"

"No thanks," Jordan managed to say. "Ummmm. Why were we looking for you? Sam, why don't you tell them?"

For once even laid-back Sam looked rattled. "We wondered if you wanted to . . . umm . . . umm . . ." His eyes met Jordan's and widened slightly.

Jordan's eyes rested on the Ocean View Art Gallery sign across the street. There was a big banner draped across the door that read Dürer.

"We wondered if you wanted to look at some woodcuts," Jordan blurted.

"Woodcuts?" Sam repeated in a puzzled tone.

Jordan jerked his head toward the sign.

Sam's eyes narrowed. His lips silently formed the word *woodcuts?*

Inwardly Jordan groaned. It was tough being the only one in the gang who knew anything about art. He began to steer the group across the street *away* from Tuxedo Tales. "Albrecht Dürer was a famous artist," he explained, his voice coming out high and thin. "His woodcuts are . . . well . . . *primo*. Right, Sam?"

"Oh, right!" Sam said, finally catching on. "Primo! A must-see. You'll laugh. You'll cry. If you only see one woodcut this season, make sure it's a Dürer."

Sky rolled her eyes. "Okay! Okay! We'll go see them. You don't have to get so manic about it."

"*Jordan!* Why are you getting so hyper?" Carrie asked as he practically pushed her across the street.

"They close early on Fridays," Jordan lied. "I want to be sure we see everything." He managed a weak chuckle and wondered if Albrecht Dürer had ever had to ask a girl to a sweet sixteen party.

Four

Sky cocked her head and stared at Ms. Farley. It was her "I'm listening intently" pose. But really and truly, she was trying to think of a tactful way to ask Rachel Harris to stop copying her.

She'd thought about it a lot over the weekend. Imitation might be the sincerest form of flattery, but this Rachel girl was taking it too far, and it was creeping Sky out.

She was going to tell Rachel—very nicely—that style was a personal thing. A self-expression thing. And that Rachel needed to learn to express her *own* personality. Sky was even going to offer to help her if she wanted. Sky loved makeovers and stuff like that. And *Clueless* was her favorite movie. Alex and Carrie had chipped in to buy her the video, and she'd watched it twenty-three and a half times. By now Sky was a makeover expert.

Ms. Farley was telling the class about the next history project. Sky was just about to mentally rehearse her tactful speech to Rachel when Ms. Farley said the magic words: "independent project."

"Independent project!" Sky whispered. She liked the way the phrase felt in her mouth. It was as satisfying as bananas and peanut butter. Two of Sky's favorite things put together.

She loved being independent.

And she loved a project.

An independent project meant Sky could use her imagination and creativity. Whatever she did, she could do it her own way.

"The project theme is Our Place in History," Ms. Farley continued.

Totally cool! Sky thought happily.

Right away Sky had about a zillion different ideas. She saw a huge map of the world superimposed over a time line. Somehow it could show how the world morphed from one big landmass called Pangaea into all the different continents and how it took millions of years, but how in the big space-time continuum those millions of years probably represented the blink of an eye.

Or maybe a big eye superimposed over a globe would get the idea across better.

No, no, no. A time line with a You Are Here and a big *X*.

Sky's pen scratched notes in the margin of her notebook. She had so many good ideas, it was going to be hard to pick just one.

"You will be working in pairs," Ms. Farley continued.

Pairs! Sky's heart sank. She put down the pen in disgust. How totally horrible. She didn't want to work with anybody else. Where was the independence if they had to work in pairs?

"Each pair will be responsible for conceiving and completing a project. Listen closely while I assign the partners." Sky shot Carrie a look, and Carrie rolled her eyes. A pair project was even worse when you didn't get to pick your own partner.

Ms. Farley reached for her notes and

began reading the names of the people who would be working together.

Sky hoped against hope that she didn't get stuck with one of The Amys—otherwise known as Number-One School Snot, Number-Two School Snot, and Number-Three School Snot.

The Amys, named for their infamous group leader, Amy Anderson, were the three most popular girls at Robert Lowell Middle School. Amy Anderson, Aimee Stewart, and Mel Eng practically ran everything at Robert Lowell—the newspaper, the student council, the bake sales, the school plays. *Everything!* It was like living under an Amy dictatorship.

Sky knew that if she wound up working with an Amy, she wouldn't have a chance. The Amys thought they knew everything. They acted like there was no such thing as a good idea if it didn't originate in an Amy brain.

Sky would have to fight to have any control at all over the project. And she would lose. Because The Amys always won. Always. That's why they were Amys. And that's why Sky and Co. couldn't stand them.

"Sky," Ms. Farley said, "you will be working with . . ."

Sky held her breath. *Please, no Amys.*

"Rachel Harris," Ms. Farley finished.

Oh no! Sky put her hand over her mouth to keep from actually groaning out loud. Rachel Harris? Her stalker?

Rachel was looking at her. She could *feel* it. She fought the impulse to turn and look, but she couldn't resist. It was like when she covered her eyes while watching *Scream* but then couldn't keep from peeking through her fingers.

Yep. There was Rachel, staring right at her. Rachel blushed when Sky's eyes met hers, but she gave her a timid smile and a tiny wave. That was when Sky noticed that Rachel had painted each one of her fingernails a different color—exactly like Sky's.

Sky waved, then turned back toward the blackboard and Ms. Farley, her mind working. On second thought, maybe she *wouldn't* have that talk with Rachel after all.

If Rachel thought everything Sky did was so great, there was no way she would argue with Sky about the project. Sky could have complete creative control.

As soon as the bell rang, Carrie rushed over to Sky and grabbed her wrist. "Tell Ms. Farley you want another partner."

"No," Sky whispered.

"Why not?" Carrie cried. "Do you want Rachel studying you up close and personal?"

"I'm not going to change partners," Sky said firmly. "It would be mean." She was sincere about that. If Rachel was so gaga over Sky, it would probably really hurt her feelings to have Sky ask for another partner.

But she was also happy to have a partner who would let Sky do the project her way.

Carrie rolled her eyes. "It's your funeral. See you in gym . . . unless Rachel gets to you first." Carrie hurried into the bustling hallway.

Sky started toward the back of the room. Rachel saw her coming and turned beet red. Sky gave Rachel her friendliest smile. "I'm glad we're going to be partners."

33

"You are?" Rachel sounded surprised.

"Sure," Sky said. "It'll be fun."

For a second Rachel looked like she thought Sky was being sarcastic or something. Like she thought maybe she was the butt of some joke.

"Come on," Sky said, trying to show her she didn't have to be afraid of her. "We can talk about it in gym class."

Rachel's eyelashes fluttered. "Seriously?"

"Sure," Sky said in a happy tone. "We can brainstorm a little while we wait in that idiot line to shoot baskets."

"I don't usually have many ideas," Rachel whispered. "I'm sure whatever you think of will be just great."

For form's sake Sky protested, but inside she knew Rachel was right. Sky would come up with a great idea. And if nobody interfered or tried to put her own two cents in, it would be the best project of all.

Sky smiled and chattered as she and Rachel walked into the locker room to get changed. But by the time they were ready to hit the basketball court, Sky was pooped. It had been a totally one-sided conversation, and she was out of breath. Rachel didn't have a word to say beyond "yes" or "no."

She could see Carrie and Sam whisper curiously to each other as she and Rachel approached the bleachers where they sat before starting exercises. "Everybody, you know Rachel Harris. Right?"

"Hi," Sam said, smiling.

"Hi," Carrie echoed, her voice chilly. "I'm not sure we have a lot of room here—"

Carrie broke off when Sky frowned at her. If Sky didn't care about Rachel imitating her, then Carrie shouldn't care, either. Carrie also needed to get over her phobia about change. There was no law that said they couldn't invite somebody new to hang with them once in a while.

". . . but I guess we can squeeze you in," Carrie added.

Seconds later Jordan and Alex came over. When Alex saw Rachel, she did a double take.

"Alex, you know Rachel, right?" Sky didn't wait for an answer. "We're working on a history project together." She arched her brows, telling Alex not to make a big deal out of Rachel being there.

Alex's face became self-consciously blank. "Cool."

"How'd the test go?" Sam asked.

Alex grinned and blew out her breath. "Not too bad. But I'm glad it's over."

"What are you going to do for your project?" Jordan asked Rachel, plopping down and adjusting the lace on his sneaker.

Rachel looked startled. "We don't know yet," she said in a flat tone. She dropped her eyes to her lap and fiddled with the hem of her shorts.

"Do you like history?" Sam asked her.

Rachel pulled at a loose thread. There was a long silence. Then Rachel looked up and realized everyone was looking at her. "Me?"

Sam smiled. "Yeah. Do you like history?"

"My grades are okay in history," Rachel answered.

"That doesn't mean you like it," Carrie said with an edge to her tone.

Rachel turned red and licked her lips. "I

guess I do. Like it, I mean. History." She trailed off, and there was another long silence as a few more kids trickled in from the locker rooms.

Sky cringed. This was getting painful. Time to turn on her gab-o-meter. "I've got tons of ideas. What do you think about this. . . ."

Rachel looked grateful to be let off the hook and sat in silence while Sky, Jordan, Sam, Alex, and Carrie laughed, joked . . . and pretty much forgot all about her.

Five

As Sky and Rachel crossed the street, headed for Ocean View's library, Sky rattled off her list of project proposals. "Now, if you don't like any of these ideas, you just have to speak up," Sky said brightly.

"Oh no," Rachel said. "They're all awesome ideas. I just . . . just . . ."

"What?" Sky asked, feeling apprehensive. She hoped she hadn't already stepped on Rachel's toes.

"I just think you should work with somebody else," Rachel said.

Uh-oh. She'd blown it. She'd been too overbearing and spooked Rachel off. Nobody wanted to be pushed around—even people who didn't seem to have much to say for themselves.

"If I did something wrong, I'm really sorry." Sky didn't want Rachel asking Ms.

Farley for another partner. Sky might wind up with somebody *really* opinionated—like an Amy.

"No," Rachel cried. "You didn't do anything wrong. I did. I'm just not . . . I don't know. I was such a moron in gym today."

"What?"

Rachel plopped down on a bench, her face screwed up against the glare of the sun. "You and your friends are like, quick, you know? Sharp. Funny."

"So?"

"So . . ." Rachel stood up again. The girl was so fidgety, Sky was sure Rachel must be on a sugar high or something. She couldn't sit still for five seconds.

"I couldn't think of anything to say," Rachel continued. "I mean . . . I *could* think of things to say . . . but I just couldn't say them. I was afraid they would come out wrong or . . . I don't know. I just think you'd be happier working with Carrie or somebody like that."

"You're not a moron," Sky said gently. She stared at Rachel and felt a surge of pity. Rachel was so shy. So awkward. Sky couldn't even begin to imagine how hard life must be for somebody who was this scared to speak.

Sky put her arm through Rachel's. "I actually like having a friend who's quiet. The rest of the gang is so gabby, it's hard to get a word in edgewise. Yak, yak, yak."

Rachel laughed. "You're just saying that because you're nice. But I know I'm a geek."

Sky stopped, realizing that she really did like Rachel. She wasn't a bump on a log. She was a person with feelings just like everybody else.

Besides, no way did Sky want another partner. A partner who might not agree with her project ideas. "You are not a geek. And I'm really happy we're going to be partners," she said. "I like having a chance to get to know somebody new."

Rachel's face looked pathetically grateful. "But I don't have any ideas at all. I'm not creative." She smiled. "I'd have to be a silent partner."

Sky laughed, surprised at the joke. "What do you mean, you don't have anything to say? That was funny. You shouldn't be so scared to talk."

Rachel shrugged. "If I looked like you, I wouldn't be."

"Huh?"

Rachel came to a stop in front of a plate glass window. "Look at me. My hair is horrible. My clothes are the worst. And my skin is the color of paste. People don't listen to what you say if they don't like the way you look."

Sky smiled. Here was her perfect chance to get Rachel to stop copying her and find an identity of her own. "Come on." She took Rachel's arm and started in the opposite direction.

"Where are we going?" Rachel cried.

"Forget the history project for now. We've got two weeks. Let's start on Project Rachel. I'm going to give you a makeover."

Rachel dug in her heels and stopped. "I can't."

"Why not?"

Rachel hung her head. "I can't afford clothes and makeup and stuff like that. My mom works real hard to support us and . . ." She trailed off.

Sky took her by the arms and forced her to look her in the eye. "Rachel Harris.

41

Listen to me. The one thing I understand is being broke. My dad's a *writer*, and my allowance is peeeuny."

Rachel giggled. "Then how do you manage to look so good all the time?"

"Two words. Vintage Voice. If you have an eye, and I've got a good one, you can pick up great stuff for nothing."

Rachel nodded. "That's my price range, all right."

Sky chuckled. When Rachel started to relax, she was quick. "Vintage Voice is around the corner," Sky said, eager to get to work. "Let's go."

As the girls crossed the square on their way to Sky's favorite store, Sky told Rachel about living on a houseboat and what it was like to have old hippies for parents. But while her mouth was talking, her mind was rearranging Rachel's straight brown hair and adding a little color to her eyes and lips.

Inside Vintage Voice, Sky breathed deeply, enjoying the aroma of old silk, faded perfume, worn leather, and mothballs.

"Wow!" Rachel said. "I've never even

been in here. It looked so cool, I was afraid to come in."

"Hey!" Sky said. "In a place like this, anything goes and everybody's welcome. Now let's think. Are you into the fifties, the sixties, the seventies, or the eighties?"

"When were scrawny, pasty-faced nerds in style?" Rachel asked in a dry tone.

Sky laughed. "Cut it out," she ordered sternly. "Think positive. Think seventies," she said. "I love the look of platforms and flared pants. You go that way. I'll go this way."

"What am I looking for?" Rachel asked in a bewildered tone.

"Stuff that's ribbed. Vests. Pants in bright colors." Sky started working her way down an aisle until she bumped into somebody. "Oh, sorry . . . Jordan?"

"Uh . . ." Jordan flushed.

"What are you doing here?" Sky asked, surprised. Jordan wasn't exactly the kind of guy who shopped for fun. He hated to shop.

He pushed his long blond bangs out of his eyes and almost dropped a bundle of clothes from his arms.

"And what are you doing with that?" Sky pointed to the black jacket and pants draped over his arm.

"Ummm, well, I've, uhh . . ." Jordan glanced around the store quickly. "I've got this sick uncle. I want to be prepared in case I have to go to a funeral. And you know I don't wear much black."

"Jordan!" Sky gasped. "I'm really sorry. How long has he been sick?"

"Oh. Not that long," Jordan answered. Sky thought he sounded kind of casual, considering. But maybe he was afraid he would start bawling if they kept talking about it.

She decided to change the subject. "Let me see," she said kindly, reaching out for the suit.

Jordan jerked away the clothes. "No! I mean . . . we don't know where it's been or who wore it. I wouldn't want you to catch anything."

"Don't be silly. If you could catch anything in here, I'd have it already." Sky smiled slightly.

But Jordan backed away. "You know, now that I think about it, he hasn't been sick all that long. I think I'll give it another week and see what happens."

"Where are you going?" Sky asked. Jordan was acting weird—even for Jordan.

"To put this back," he said over his shoulder.

"Wow!" Rachel appeared on the other side of the rack. "Does he always act so nervous?"

Sky shook her head. "No. I guess he's really upset."

"Think we should do anything?" Rachel asked.

"I don't really know what we could do," Sky said thoughtfully. "I'll call him tonight and make sure he's okay. In the meantime, let's get to work on you."

Rachel grinned—the biggest smile Sky had ever seen from her before. It lit up her face and made her look almost pretty.

Sky smiled and started rifling through the racks. This makeover might not be such hard work after all.

Six

"Talk about close," Jordan muttered. He collapsed on a bench around the corner from the Vintage Voice, his forehead wet with sweat. He lifted his sleeve, wiped his face, and looked around for Sam, hoping he got the message Jordan had left on his machine.

Right on time, Sam flew around the corner on his skateboard. "I guess you're wondering why I called you here," Jordan joked in his James Bond voice.

"Another tuxedo nonshopping experience?" Sam popped up his board and caught it with his right hand.

"It was. But Sky's in there, so it's a no-go for today," Jordan admitted.

Sam slumped down on the bench and placed his board down next to him. "Did she want to know what you were doing in there?" Sam asked.

"I told her some lame story about needing something to wear to a funeral."

Sam laughed. "Whose?"

"My imaginary uncle's." Jordan hung his head. "It's a good thing I'm not considering a career as a spy. Covert operations are too hard on my system."

"Seriously, dude." Sam shook his head. "That is one lame story."

"I know. I *hate* lying," Jordan said. "It just gives me major BO." He sniffed his shirt for emphasis and grimaced. "It would have been so much easier if I could have just said, 'I'm going to this formal party. Why don't you come?'"

"So do it," Sam urged. "No matter what you do, you've got trouble, so you might as well get it over with and ask Sky."

"Yeah, right. And by tomorrow morning Carrie will be sticking pins in a Jordan voodoo doll. And Alex'll probably try to run me over with her skateboard."

"Maybe not," Sam mused. "Alex is a tomboy. She probably wouldn't even *want* to go to a fancy sweet sixteen party."

Jordan nodded. "True. And Carrie hates anything fussy or fancy. It reminds her of her mother. She wouldn't want to go, either. So there's really no problem. Right?"

"Right," both boys said in a positive tone.

They looked at each other.

"Wrong," they both groaned.

"It's not the party they're going to care about," Sam said. "It's the choosing one girl over the others. They're going to care about that big-time."

"That's it!" Jordan slumped back in the seat. "I'm doomed! Don't be surprised if I don't show up for school tomorrow and in two weeks you get a postcard from Africa. I'm going home, packing a bag, and hitching the next flight outta here."

"Sure, man," Sam said, standing and hopping onto his skateboard. "Call you tonight?"

"Sure," Jordan replied.

"Jordan! Telephone!" Mr. Sullivan's voice managed to penetrate the fog around Jordan's brain. He put the finishing touches on his cartoon, shut the pad, and went out to the phone in the hall. "Hello?"

"Hi, Jordan. It's Sky. I was just calling to see how your uncle is doing."

"Uncle?" Jordan began. "What un—" He broke off, remembering his stupid lie. "Ummm . . . believe it or not, he's fine. He made a complete recovery this afternoon."

"Really? That's great," Sky said. "So is this your mom's brother or your dad's?"

"Neither," Jordan said before he had a chance to think. "I mean, he's really a family friend, so we call him uncle, but he's not related. He's not even that close. He doesn't even live in this country. He lives in Australia, and we haven't seen him for years."

"Then how did you know he got sick?" Sky asked. "And that he got better?"

Yeah, moron. How did you know? Jordan thought. "E-mail," he said, trying desperately to think of a way to change the subject.

His parents' bedroom door opened. Mrs. Sullivan stuck her head out the door. "Who is that?" she whispered.

"Sky," he mouthed.

"Ask her," Mrs. Sullivan hissed.

Jordan clapped his hand over the phone so Sky couldn't hear. "Mom! Please!"

Mrs. Sullivan narrowed her eyes but retreated back into her bedroom.

"Jordan? Are you there?"

"Yeah. But I gotta go. My mother is . . . um . . . my mother is sick."

"Oh no. What's the matter with her?"

"Same thing my uncle had," Jordan said, feeling like a total idiot. "But it's one of those personal and embarrassing kinds of illnesses, so don't ask her about it if you see her, okay? Bye!"

Jordan hung up the phone, breathing heavily.

Why did Cousin Margaret have to have a sweet sixteen party? he wondered miserably. Why . . . why . . . why . . . why . . . why?

Tuesday

MRS. SULLIVAN:	"Did you get a tux?"
JORDAN SULLIVAN:	"No, but I will."
MRS. S.:	"Did you ask a girl?"
JORDAN:	"No, but I will."
MRS. S.:	"Jordan, I'm counting on you."
JORDAN:	"I know, Mom. I won't let you down."

Wednesday

MRS. S. (TENSE):	"Did you get a tux?"
JORDAN:	"Uh . . . no, but I will."
MRS. S. (TENSER STILL):	"Did you ask a girl?"
JORDAN:	"No, but I—"
MRS. S.:	"Your brothers have already rented their tuxes and invited lovely girls."
JORDAN (FUMBLING):	"I've been busy. I had a test. My stomach hurts. I'll do it tomorrow."

Thursday

MRS. S.:	"Did you get a tux?"
JORDAN:	"No, but I—"
MRS. S.:	"I don't want to hear another

word out of you until you've rented one."

JORDAN: "I—"

(MRS. SULLIVAN FIXES HIM WITH A THREATENING GLARE. JORDAN SHUTS UP.)

Friday

MRS. S.: "Did you get a tux?"

JORDAN: "Um . . ."

MRS. S.: "Are you *trying* to kill me? Are you *trying* to break my heart? Do I ask so much that—"

JORDAN: "Tomorrow. I'll go tomorrow."

MRS. S.: "Your aunt Carla is going to be there. Her brothers are going to be there. Her ex-husbands are going to be there—all three of them, including the one with the Mercedes dealership. I want my sons to look their best. I want everyone to see the five Sullivan boys and say—"

JORDAN: "Look at the cute little guy in the monkey suit. Where's

	the organ-grinder?"
MRS. S.:	"Don't be smart!"
JORDAN:	"Sorry, Mom. I'll get the tux tomorrow. I promise."
MRS. S.:	"Don't come home without it."
JORDAN:	"Yes, ma'am."

Seven

"Stand still!" Sky ordered.

"I can't. I'm too excited." Rachel stood in front of the mirror while Sky pulled in the waistband of a vintage skirt.

"How's that?" Sky asked.

Rachel frowned. "It depends. Am I supposed to be able to breathe in this?"

Sky laughed and loosened her grip a couple of inches.

Rachel took a deep breath. "Perfect!"

"Okay. Take it off, and I'll sew it."

Rachel slipped out of the skirt, and Sky took it over to her bed, where she had spread out her stack of old fashion magazines. Sky called them her "archives," and her mom called them "that junk under the bed."

"I can't believe you did all this in just a week," Rachel marveled.

Sky had taken the few sad garments

Rachel possessed, added their incredibly good haul from Vintage Voice, and worked some patented Sky Foley magic.

"Where did this come from?" Rachel asked, holding up a cropped black tailored jacket.

Sky laughed. "Remember that blazer you thought was so gross? I cleaned it up, cut the length, and sewed on some new buttons. It'll look great with flared jeans and boots."

"You're amazing!" Rachel said. "I feel like Cinderella."

Sky smiled. "That's cool. Because I like being a fairy godmother."

"Next to you, Cinderella's godmother was a slacker," Rachel joked. "She had a wand. I mean, how hard did she have to work? You do it the old-fashioned way—with a needle and thread."

Sky crossed her legs and settled herself more comfortably. "It's nice to be appreciated," she said with a smile.

"Don't your friends appreciate you?" Rachel asked, a shadow crossing her face.

"I don't know," Sky began. "Carrie always wears black and can pretty much buy what she wants, so she doesn't think much about it. Alex isn't into clothes. She wears the stuff her older brother outgrows. Jordan and Sam are guys. So . . ." Sky shrugged. "I don't really have any friends who are into being creative—fashionwise, I mean. Carrie is a very creative writer. And Jordan is an artist."

"Where did you learn to sew?" Rachel asked, watching Sky as she put the finishing touches on the skirt.

"My mom taught me. You could learn."

Rachel twisted a metal bracelet on her wrist. "I could learn to sew. But I could never have the *ideas* you have."

"That's a pretty bracelet," Sky commented. "Where did you get it?"

"I made it," Rachel said.

"You're kidding." Sky was shocked.

"No. I did it in art class."

"What is it made of?" Sky asked.

Rachel started laughing. "I don't know. It's something that fell off my mom's car."

Sky began to laugh so hard, she choked. "I can relate. I once made a flowerpot out of my mom's dead coffeemaker."

The two girls started comparing stories

and couldn't stop laughing. Pretty soon Sky fell back on the bed and Rachel rolled on the floor, holding her stomach, she was laughing so hard.

"You're the first person I ever felt like I could tell something like that," Rachel gasped.

Sky sat up and watched Rachel pull herself together, realizing how much she liked her. "We're probably the only two people at Robert Lowell Middle School who could see how funny that is." She finally caught her breath. "That bracelet is majorly cool. So why are you running yourself down, saying you don't have any talent?"

"I don't know. Habit, I guess. You really like it?" Rachel asked.

"Yes!"

Rachel took it off and handed it to Sky. "Then I want you to have it."

Sky took the bracelet and turned it over, admiring it. Then she handed it back to Rachel. "I can't take it. But thanks for offering."

"Why?" Rachel asked.

Sky stared at Rachel's simple, trusting

face. Sky had been to Rachel's house. Rachel had almost nothing. There was no way Sky was going to take away her only cool bracelet. But Sky knew that poor girls had their pride.

"Because it's so perfect with these," Sky said. She jumped off the bed and took something out of the closet. A pair of red silk pajama bottoms with silver embroidery.

"No way!" Rachel squeaked. "I'd never have the nerve to wear those."

"So start with the jeans and the jacket and work your way up," Sky said with a laugh.

Rachel took the pants from Sky. Her lip trembled a little. "Why are you doing this for me?" she asked.

"Because I like you," Sky said.

"That's a first," Rachel whispered.

Sky felt her face flush guiltily. It wasn't as if she was being completely unselfish. Sure, she wanted to make Rachel's life easier, but she also wanted to make sure Rachel was one hundred percent bowled over by Sky so Sky could do what she wanted with the history project.

"Hey! I practiced with the makeup," Rachel said excitedly. "Want me to show you?"

"Sure!" Sky said, glad that Rachel was acting so lively. It was a welcome change.

Sky had cleaned out her makeup drawer and put together a box of samples, extras, and discards for Rachel. She'd also given Rachel all kinds of makeup tips.

So far Rachel hadn't had the nerve to appear at school wearing any makeup. But now that she had the great wardrobe, Sky hoped she'd be psyched to go all the way.

Sky pulled out her latest copy of *Teen View* magazine and flopped on the bed. "Oh, good. I love these. Here's a 'Test Your Personality' quiz."

She settled down to take the quiz while Rachel worked on her face.

1. You and a friend are on your way to a party. She puts on a dress that makes her look like a total dog. You:

   a. Tell her she barks;

   b. Tactfully ask her where her darling green outfit is;

   c. Tell her you know fashion is about

feeling good—and ask her how she feels about what she is wearing.

2. *You and a friend are on your way to a party. She puts on a dress that makes you look like a total dog compared to her. You:*

  a. Bark, and then congratulate her on looking so outstanding;
  b. Tactfully ask her where her darling green outfit is;
  c. Tell her you know fashion is about feeling good—and that you feel horrible about what she is wearing.

3. *Your friend needs help. You help her out because:*

  a. You're a friend, and that's what friends do;
  b. You want something from her and figure this way, she can't tell you no;
  c. You're too gutless to say no.

Sky closed the magazine. She wasn't too crazy about this quiz after all.

"What do you think?" Rachel asked.

Sky looked up and gasped. It was

amazing. Pasty-faced Rachel Harris looked totally glam.

"You look great," Sky said, feeling proud of herself. She'd turned an ugly duckling into a swan.

Rachel blinked at Sky. "I've never had any friends before. Thank you." Then she backed away. "I'm sorry. We're not actually friends, right? I mean, you're only hanging out with me because of the project."

Sky rolled her eyes. Talk about low self-esteem! If Rachel could just stop thinking of herself as a worthless worm, she wouldn't seem like such a nerd.

"That's why we *started* hanging out, but that's not why we're friends," Sky said. "We are friends, aren't we?"

Rachel's eyes shone. And Sky realized that with or without makeup, Rachel Harris was pretty. Really pretty. All it took to bring it out was a little happiness. A little self-confidence. And a little attention.

Eight

"Jordan! Is that you?" Mrs. Sullivan appeared at the head of the stairs. She looked down with hard eyes and a pinched mouth.

"It's me," he answered, closing the door behind him. "Ta da!" He whisked the vintage tux from behind his back and waved it like a matador's cape. He'd gotten Sam to stand guard at the door of the shop this morning while Jordan tried it on. Fortunately none of the girls had come by.

His mother started down the stairs, her nose wrinkling. "What on earth is that?"

"It's a tux. A quality tux. A tux that's probably hung out with crowned heads of Europe. Movie stars. Maybe even international spies," Jordan said proudly.

His mother took the jacket and pants from him gingerly as if she expected them to fall apart at the seams. But when she shook them out and held them up, a slow smile spread over her face. "Jordan," she said happily. "What would I do without you? You *do* have taste. Once this is cleaned and pressed, it's going to be perfect."

Jordan breathed a sigh of relief. "Okay. Well. Good. Then that's that." He started up the stairs. "I'll, uh . . ."

"Hold it!"

Jordan froze. He knew what was coming.

"Which one of those cute girls did you invite?"

Cute girls? Carrie, Alex, and Sky?

He never really thought of them as cute girls. They were more like buddies. Still, it was best to humor her right now.

"They are cute, aren't they?" he said, hoping to distract her. "Did I tell you what Sky said to me the other day?"

"You asked Sky?" his mother said happily.

"Well . . ."

"Carrie?"

"Well . . ."

"Alex?"

"Hey! One thing at a time. I got the tux."

"One tux does not a sweet sixteen party make," his mother shot back. "You need a girl."

"Nobody *needs* a girl," he reasoned. "I mean, we don't have any girls around here, and we're doing just fine."

That did it.

"Jordan Sullivan!" his mother shouted. "I've had just about all the nonsense I'm going to take from you. If you don't—"

Jordan took to the stairs, running for cover. "Okay. Okay. I'll do it. But I've got to think about it."

"What's to think about?" she called after him. "Just call somebody up and—"

Blam!

Jordan slammed the door to his room and began to pace.

Carrie? Alex? Sky?

Alex? Sky? Carrie?

Sky? Carrie? Alex?

He threw himself facedown on the bed, closed his eyes, and picked a name out of his mental hat. Alex! Hmmm . . .

Jordan and Alex Go to the Party

A Screenplay by
Jordan Sullivan's Overactive Imagination

FADE IN:

INT: COUNTRY CLUB

JORDAN *enters a large ballroom filled with people in tuxedos and cocktail dresses.*

> MRS. SULLIVAN
> Jordan? I told you to bring a girl.

> JORDAN
> I did. Here she comes now. Gangway!

SFX: SKIDDING WHEELS
CLOSE ON: MRS. SULLIVAN

> MRS. SULLIVAN
> Oh no!

ALEX *comes skateboarding into the ballroom, going full speed. The crowd scatters in order to avoid collision. ALEX hits the edge of the dance platform and goes airborne.*
ANGLE ON: THE ICE SCULPTURE
CLOSE ON: JORDAN
He covers his eyes.

CLOSE ON: MRS. SULLIVAN
She reacts as . . .

ALEX *hits the ice sculpture. The board goes one way. ALEX goes another. The ice sculpture hits the ballroom floor.*

SFX: CRASH

JORDAN *watches in helpless horror. One by one* THE GUESTS *begin gathering around him. Their faces are angry.* MRS. SULLIVAN *pushes her way through the crowd to confront* JORDAN.

> MRS. SULLIVAN
> You idiot! You've ruined everything. From now on you are not my son.

CLOSE ON: COUSIN MARGARET

> COUSIN MARGARET
> And you're not my first cousin, either.

MARGARET *bursts into tears and runs off camera.*
MRS. SULLIVAN *bursts into tears and runs off camera.*
MR. SULLIVAN *bursts into tears and runs off camera.*
Jordan's FOUR BROTHERS *burst into tears and run off camera.*
Everybody else bursts into tears and runs off camera.*
JORDAN *is left standing alone in the middle of the empty ballroom.*

FADE OUT

Jordan and Carrie Go to the Party

A Screenplay by
Jordan Sullivan's Fevered Mind

FADE IN:

INT: THE COUNTRY CLUB

JORDAN *and* CARRIE *enter* COUSIN MARGARET's *sweet sixteen party.* JORDAN *wears a vintage tuxedo.* CARRIE *wears something vaguely shroudlike and a corsage of black flowers. They join the receiving line.*

COUSIN MARGARET
  Jordan! I'm so happy to see you. This must be Carrie.

MARGARET *extends her hand to* CARRIE. *Instead of shaking it* CARRIE *turns it over and examines* MARGARET's *palm, reading it.* CARRIE *gasps, then shakes her head.*

CARRIE
  I see some really heinous stuff in your future.

COUSIN MARGARET
  Well, like, did you have to tell me *today?* At my sweet sixteen party? You couldn't wait until *tomorrow?*

JORDAN *and* CARRIE *continue along the receiving line. But* CARRIE *will not shake anybody's hand. Instead she reads each palm, making terrible predictions as she works her way down the receiving line.*

                    CARRIE
   Your teeth are going to fall out. . . .
Your boyfriend is going to break up with
you. . . . You're going to step in dog
doo. . . .

Jordan's FOUR BROTHERS *converge around* CARRIE.

                    BROTHER #1
   Knock   it   off.   You're   bumming
everybody out.

                    JORDAN
   Don't mess with her. It's dangerous.

                    BROTHER #2
   Out of the way, runt. We're throwing
your gloomy gal pal out.

BROTHERS #3 *and* #4 *each take one of* CARRIE's *arms.*
                    JORDAN
(screams)
   Noooo!

Too late the brothers realize that CARRIE *isn't just depressing, she's also telekinetic!*
CARRIE *nods.*

SFX: EXPLOSIONS

BROTHERS #3 *and* #4 *fly backward and hit the wall.*

CARRIE *nods again.*

SFX: AIRPLANES
A V formation of pickle forks comes flying across the room. They buzz the guests before targeting BROTHERS #1 *and* #2, *who run from the room, screaming.*

CARRIE
(diabolical laughter)

MRS. SULLIVAN *bursts into tears.*

                    MRS. SULLIVAN
(tearful)
  Oh, Jordan. Why couldn't you have asked some nice girl? You've just ruined everything.

FADE OUT

Jordan and Sky Go to the Party

A Screenplay by Jordan Sullivan
(Written before he ran away to Africa)

FADE IN:

INT: THE COUNTRY CLUB

SKY *dances across the floor. She looks beautiful. She smiles. She laughs. Everyone begins to look at her with admiring eyes.*

PULL BACK TO REVEAL . . .
. . . *her dancing partner is one of Jordan's* BROTHERS.

CUT TO:

INT: BACK OF THE BALLROOM

JORDAN *sits at a large table by himself. He crumbles a roll and watches the dancers with a sad face.* MRS. SULLIVAN *sits down beside him.*

> MRS. SULLIVAN
> Jordan! That Sky is a doll. Everybody thinks she's the greatest thing since sliced bread. So friendly. So outgoing. And she's danced every dance.

JORDAN

Right! And she's danced with every single person here—except me.

MRS. SULLIVAN *shrugs.*

MRS. SULLIVAN
(breezy)

Well! That's the price you pay for bringing such a cute girl.

CLOSE ON JORDAN:
He drops his head into his hands and groans.

FADE OUT

Nine

I wonder how I would look as a blonde.

Sky sat on the deck of the houseboat, flipping through the fashion and beauty section of the local paper. Making Rachel over had given her the itch to do something dramatic to her own looks. Then her eyes landed on an ad straight out of her dreams.

FREE CUTS AT THE OCEAN VIEW BEAUTY COLLEGE. ONE DAY ONLY.

"Whooaaa!" Sky bent her head to see if there was any fine print she ought to know about—like that you had to buy a gazillion dollars' worth of shampoo to get the free cut.

Nope. It looked like the real deal. A free cut with no strings attached.

"All right!" Sky jumped up and started

toward the phone to call Carrie or Alex. She picked up the receiver, then put it back down.

Carrie would go if Sky asked her to, but no way would she change her long, dyed black hairdo. And unless Sky was going for a goth look, Carrie wasn't going to get too excited sitting around a beauty school. She'd probably just sit there making sarcastic remarks about people's hair and wind up making the stylist so mad, she would take it out on Sky and shave her head or something.

Nope. This wasn't Carrie's kind of field trip.

Alex? She would also go if Sky asked her to. But she would be totally bored and wind up skateboarding around the salon until they kicked her out.

Nope. Sky had only one friend who would be into going with Sky to get a new look.

She dialed Rachel's number.

"Hello?"

Sky smiled. Already Rachel's voice sounded more confident. "It's me. Sky."

"Wow! I usually only get phone calls from telemarketing companies."

Sky laughed. "Things change. Wanna meet me at the beauty school? They're doing free cuts today."

"Uh-oh," Rachel said. "What are you going to do to me?"

"You could use a trim. And I'm going to do something wild and crazy."

"What did you have in mind? Dreads? Highlights?"

Sky smiled. It was nice having somebody express genuine interest in her hair. "I think I'll decide when I get there. Can you meet me?"

"Let me check my calendar."

Sky laughed.

"Let's see," Rachel said in her dry, funny voice. "I did promise Amy Anderson I'd go shopping with her. Then I'm supposed to be interviewed on KHOP. After that I have a fashion shoot. But I guess I could fit you in. What time?"

"I'm leaving now," Sky said.

"Okay. I'm on my way. And Sky . . ."

"Yeah?"

"Thanks."

"For what?"

"You know. Asking me to come."

Sky smiled. "See ya there." Sky replaced the receiver, ran back up the stairs, and saw her dad getting in the car. "Dad!" she yelled. "Wait." She ran across the dock up to the road and hopped in the passenger side. "Will you drive me to Old Town Square?"

Mr. Foley grinned. "Do I have a choice?"

"No. It's an emergency," Sky said urgently.

"Ohhhh," Mr. Foley said, his voice full of mirth. "Are we going to the hospital?"

"No." Sky giggled. "The beauty school. They're giving free haircuts."

"Well, why didn't you say so?" Mr. Foley gasped. He honked the horn, executed a reckless U-turn, and gunned the old engine. The car backfired.

Sky laughed. Neither one of her parents had any fashion sense, but they did have good senses of humor.

Sky hopped out of the car as soon as they reached the square. "Bye. Thanks."

"Don't do anything you'll regret in the morning," he called out with a laugh. "I'll be at the museum if you need a ride back."

As Sky hurried to the beauty school she heard her dad's car chugging away. That *car* belonged in a museum, she reflected. It *was* a museum—covered with peace, love, and hippieness bumper stickers and full of artifacts from her parents' past. Her parents had driven that junk heap across the country when they were eighteen. The thing was like a time capsule on four wheels.

"That's it!" she said out loud, opening the door to the beauty school. "That's it. That's the idea!"

Rachel was waiting just inside the door. "Are you talking to me or to yourself?"

Sky took Rachel by the shoulders and shook her happily. "I've got a great idea for our history project. A time capsule."

Rachel's face went blank.

Sky forced herself to slow down. "A time capsule. A time capsule. How do I explain this? You take stuff that's meaningful, that says something about you and the world you live in, and you seal it up. Then in a hundred years people in the future can open it and see what you were like."

Rachel's face began to beam. "I get it. I know exactly what you're talking about. That's so cool! What would we put in it?"

Sky's brain was working overtime. "Jordan's cartoons. A couple of Carrie's short stories. Alex's competition ribbons. Sam's Native American artifacts."

Rachel tweaked Sky's braids. "One of these!"

A stylist motioned to Sky that she was free. Sky practically skipped over to the chair and hopped up into it. The stylist excused herself to go get a plastic bib.

Sky smiled at her reflection in the mirror and saw Rachel's face.

It had ceased to beam. In fact, it looked a little angry.

Sky's heart thumped. Uh-oh. Was Rachel going to say she didn't like the idea? Try to start messing with Sky's concept? She swallowed and made sure there was no antagonism in her voice. "Don't you like the idea?"

Rachel paused, then nodded.

"What's wrong, then?"

Rachel bit her lower lip. "Can't I put something in the time capsule?"

Sky let out her breath in a gust of relief. "Oh, is that all?" Sky gave herself a mental kick for leaving Rachel out.

But she wished Rachel would have just spoken up instead of looking like she'd been kicked and making Sky feel guilty. "Of course you can put something in," Sky said tightly. "It is *our* project. What would you like to include?"

Rachel's face began to beam again. "Maybe I'll make another bracelet and put it in there since you think the first one is cool."

Sky's irritation evaporated. How could she get annoyed with Rachel? It would be like smacking a totally harmless, completely well-meaning puppy.

Sky sat back in the chair, wondering what kind of magic or miracle it would take to give Rachel more backbone.

Later that evening the phone rang, and Sky picked it up. "Hello?"

"Hi. It's me. Carrie. Remember? Carrie Mersel. The friend you've hardly seen in a week."

Sky leaned back. "Sorry about that. I've been busy. You know, on a project."

"With Rachel?" Carrie's voice was flat and disapproving.

"Yeah. She's turning out to be really nice."

"You are *so* naive," Carrie said impatiently.

"Why are you so negative about Rachel?" Sky demanded.

"Because I don't trust her," Carrie said. "I don't trust people who copy other people. Copying your style would be like somebody copying one of my stories."

"Well, she's not going to copy me anymore," Sky said.

"What do you mean?" Carrie somehow sounded even more suspicious.

"She's got her own style now. You'll see," Sky promised.

"I'll believe it when I see it. You've made us sit with her every single day at lunch, and she doesn't have one word to say."

"She's intimidated!" Sky argued.

"What's so intimidating about us?" Carrie demanded.

"Maybe it's you giving her dirty looks," Sky suggested.

"I do not."

"You do too."

"When?" Carrie demanded.

"Only every time she looks like she's going to say something," Sky retorted. "Of course she clams up when you look at her like that!"

"Did Rachel tell you this?" Carrie asked angrily.

"No. I noticed it all by myself," Sky said lightly. "Now chill out, would you? And do me a favor—be nice to her. Okay? It's important to me."

Carrie sighed. "Okay. But only because you're asking me as a favor. So I'm going to get a big surprise tomorrow?"

Sky smiled to herself and ran her hands through her new, outrageously short hair. "You're going to get a couple of surprises," she promised.

Monday Morning Face-off

Mrs. Sullivan faced Jordan from behind the kitchen counter like a steely-eyed gunslinger.

Jordan forced himself to meet his mother's gaze. He began to tremble. He was fast, and he was good. That youngest Sullivan boy was known for his quick comebacks and rapid-fire reflexes.

But he was outgunned, and he knew it.

His mother had more firepower. In the blink of an eye she could withhold his allowance, ground him, or bar his access to the TV. On top of all that, she had the keys to the car.

"Jordan," she said in a gravelly tone.

"Yes, Mom?"

"The party is in less than a week. I have to turn in your guest's name so the hostess can put it on her place card. You have until sundown."

Jordan gulped. "Yes, ma'am."

The horn honked. Grateful for an excuse to end this conversation, Jordan ran from the kitchen and outside, where he took several deep, bracing gulps of fresh air.

He climbed onto the bus, said hello to Brick, and hurried to the back. "Where's Sky?"

Carrie leaned over Alex and Sam. "Her mom came out and said her dad was driving her to school later. And that's good because I want to talk about her behind her back."

"Carrie!" Sam warned.

"It's nothing bad," Carrie said. "I just want to tell everybody to be nice to Rachel Harris or else."

Alex laughed. "Or else what?"

"Or else I'll write a tasty little story about you and publish it in the paper."

"Nooooo!" they all screamed, laughing. Carrie slammed hard when she slammed in writing.

Sam laughed. "Why are you telling *us* to be nice? We're always nice. You're the one who has the big problem with Rachel."

"I still have a problem with Rachel. But Sky's put a lot of effort into remodeling Rachel—or whatever it is you call it."

"Remodeling?" Sam asked. "What is she, a Buick?"

"I'm guessing she means a makeover," Alex said. "Okay. We'll make a big fuss. Even if she looks weird. Has anybody seen her? I mean, do we know what Sky did to her? Sky *does* get carried away sometimes."

"It doesn't matter," Carrie said. "The point is, act impressed. Not for Rachel. For Sky."

Jordan looked out the window, wishing that being nice to Rachel Harris was the only challenging thing he had to do today. Somehow he was going to have to figure out who to ask to the sweet sixteen party, and he was going to have to do it fast.

Countdown to Lunchtime

11:10 A.M. Sam's stomach rumbles very loudly. Mel Eng gives him a dirty look. To take his mind off food, Sam practices making imaginary one-sided conversation with Rachel. It's hard. But he's willing to do it—for Sky's sake.

11:20 A.M. Carrie makes a list of nice things to say to Rachel Harris. It's a short list: one entry so far—*Hi, Rachel. How are you?*—but there's still thirty minutes left. She's sure she can come up with *something*.

11:30 A.M. Alex sneaks a peek into her lunch bag to do a last minute cookie count. She made chocolate chip cookies over the weekend and brought them in to share. But she wants to make sure she

84

has enough for everyone, including Rachel. She doesn't need a Carrie-style, publicized roasting.

11:45 A.M. Jordan wishes he were dead.

11:50 A.M. The lunch bell tolls. It's party time.

Ten

A few minutes after noon Sky hurried toward her locker. Just as she had hoped, the halls were empty. Everyone was already at lunch.

"Where have you been?" a voice behind her cried.

Sky turned. Rachel Harris stepped out from behind the lockers. She wore the black cropped jacket with some flared jeans. Her face was all made up, and her freshly trimmed hair hung perfectly straight down her back. She looked amazing.

"At the dentist," Sky lied. She'd actually faked a stomachache that morning so she could remain unseen by anyone until lunch. She wanted to go into the cafeteria a little late and make a dramatic entrance.

"Why aren't you at lunch?" Sky asked.

"I didn't have the nerve to go into the

cafeteria alone," Rachel said with a nervous laugh. "How do I look?"

Sky stood back and inspected Rachel. "Watch out, Niki Taylor," she said with a grin.

"Seriously?" Rachel asked, groaning. "I'm so nervous, I didn't want anybody to see me. I faked a stomachache and spent the morning in the nurse's office."

Sky sucked in her breath. Whoaaa. Rachel had started out *looking* like Sky and now she was *thinking* like Sky. "You mean nobody's seen you?" Sky asked.

Rachel shook her head. "No. So we'll be making our debuts together."

Sky felt an unfamiliar stab of irritation. This wasn't what she had planned at all. Her own new look was so dramatic, so out there and cool, she wanted to walk into the cafeteria alone and see if people even recognized her.

"What's wrong?" Rachel asked warily.

Sky felt ashamed of herself for letting her annoyance show. "No . . . I mean, nothing. Come on. Let's go eat lunch."

Sky took a last look at her cropped mop and giggled. What difference did it make if she walked into the cafeteria with Rachel? This look was a real attention getter. It was going to solidify Sky Foley's position on the Robert Lowell style map.

Her heart beat a little faster as they neared the cafeteria. She couldn't wait to see her friends' faces. Alex would pull her cap down over her face as if she was so amazed, she couldn't look. Jordan would be too stunned to think up a friendly insult. And Sam would undoubtedly whistle.

The noise from the cafeteria sounded unusually loud as they walked in. As Sky moved through the crowded cafeteria with Rachel she could hear people whispering to each other.

She tried not to smile.

When she spotted the gang, they were laughing and talking. Carrie was just about to take a bite out of her sandwich when she looked up. She froze in midbite. One by one each of Sky's friends broke off their conversation and looked at her.

Jordan's eyes almost bugged out, and Sam's mouth dropped open. Alex took off her cap and twirled it around. Carrie smiled—slightly.

Sam was the first to say anything.

"You look great!"

Alex pulled her cap back on and grinned. "Unbelievable."

Jordan stood up and bowed in a comical fashion. "Rachel, I'm not worthy," he said, raising his eyebrows in a parody of cool.

Rachel?

That was when Sky realized that not one pair of eyes was focused on her. They were all focused on something *behind* her. Rachel Harris, to be exact.

Rachel stepped past Sky and pulled out a chair. "Thank you," she said, blushing a little.

Carrie nodded. "You look good," she said.

"Model good," Alex added. "Did you cut your hair?"

"If *I'd* cut my hair, it would look like a mop," she joked. "No. The lady at the beauty school cut it."

"The beauty school! Good choice! That's a major bargain," Carrie said.

Sky waited for Rachel to tell Carrie it had been Sky's idea. But Rachel didn't say anything.

Alex reached into her pack. "Here, Rach. I made some cookies. Have one."

Rach? They were going to have nicknames now?

Sky pulled out a chair and sat. Collapsed, really. It was as if nobody had even noticed that she had gotten a haircut.

Rachel took the cookie, broke off half, and handed the other half back to Alex. "I'd better not eat the whole thing. These jeans are pretty tight—the ultimate hip shaper."

The guys laughed, and even Carrie smiled. A real smile. Not a grimacing smile.

Rachel looked pleased to have gotten a reaction.

"So where were you all morning?" Carrie asked.

Sky started to tell them the lie about her dental appointment, but before she could answer, Rachel piped in, "The nurse's office."

Carrie wasn't talking to you, Rachel, Sky thought resentfully.

But apparently she was.

"What's wrong?" they all asked Rachel, their faces concerned.

"Nothing," Rachel joked. "Just stage fright."

The gang laughed again.

Sky decided it was time to assert herself. "I had to go to the dentist this morning, and—"

"I have terrible stage fright," Jordan said, cutting Sky off as if he hadn't heard a word. "One year I had a solo in the school play, and I thought I was going to pass out."

"I hate oral reports," Alex said. "Center stage isn't for me."

Sky fidgeted miserably with her necklace. She *did* like center stage. But Rachel had taken that spot and was holding her own.

Nobody had said word one about Sky's outrageous haircut. Had they even noticed?

Or maybe the cut had been a huge mistake. Maybe it was just so horrible that nobody knew what to say, so they weren't saying anything at all.

Suddenly Sky was sick with humiliation and regret. What had possessed her? Had she lost her mind? Her hair had always been one of her best features.

Now she had ruined her looks—and created a monster of competition called Rachel Harris.

Rachel's cheeks were pink, and her eyes were sparkling. It was obvious that she was blossoming under the attention and admiration.

"So now that you're all dressed up, where are you going to go?" Jordan asked Rachel.

"Oh, I was thinking I might make an appearance in history class," Rachel answered in a mock-snobby voice, thrusting her nose in the air. They all laughed—*again*.

"Excuse me," Sky said. "I'm going to get a drink." Desperate to get away, she hopped up and disappeared into the cafeteria line. She bypassed the people waiting for food and went to the end, where the beverage stand was. She filled a paper cup with ice, then held it under the water dispenser. The ice rattled in the cup, and she realized with a start that her hands were shaking.

"Cutting your hair with the vacuum cleaner these days?" Amy Anderson asked snidely as she passed by with her tray.

Sky was so embarrassed, her shaking wrist went limp and the cup full of ice water slipped from her hand. It hit the floor with a loud smack. Ice and water spewed out in every direction.

There was a long, sudden silence, as there always was when something was dropped, then applause and jeers.

"Way to go, hedgehog girl!" somebody shouted.

Salty tears stung Sky's eyes. Her cheeks were so hot, she felt as if she might actually faint. Instead she hurried toward the door. She had to get out of there. She had to get some air.

Between the cafeteria and the school building was a covered walkway. There was a ladies' room along there that nobody ever used because it didn't get heat from the main building. That meant it was cold. So nobody used it unless they had to barf or something.

Sky had discovered it in fifth grade. It was a great place to hide and lick wounds after being attacked in the cafeteria.

The last time she had been there was seventh grade, after two girls had told her she smelled like garlic and asked her to move to another table.

She'd hoped that her postcafeteria wound-licking days were over.

Apparently she was wrong.

Eleven

"I think that went well," Jordan said. Rachel had run off to get something out of her locker while the rest of the class went out for recess.

"I think it went great," Sam said. "And it wasn't even hard."

Alex nodded. "Yeah. She talks now. It makes a big difference."

Jordan bent to tie his shoe. "She doesn't just talk; she makes jokes. I mean, she's quick."

"I guess Sky really knows how to bring people out of their shells," Sam said. "We need to tell her she did a great job. Where is Sky, anyway?"

"I guess she went table hopping to show off her haircut," Carrie said with a laugh. "I never did get a chance to tell her she looks cool. I was working the Rachel thing."

Suddenly Jordan had a brilliant idea. Rachel Harris had just presented a fourth option in the sweet sixteen dilemma. An option that would make him look good, make Sky happy, and keep him out of hot water. He had to find her—pronto.

"I'll see you guys later," he said.

"Where are you going?" Carrie asked.

"Gotta do some stuff," Jordan answered. He hurried out of the cafeteria. Rachel was in the walkway, just about to open the door to the building.

"Rachel! Wait up."

Rachel stopped and turned around with a look of surprise on her face. "Were you calling me?"

Jordan was struck again by how changed she seemed. Her cheeks were a little pink, like they were when she was embarrassed, but she was looking him right in the eye—which was kind of unnerving since she looked so pretty.

Jordan almost chickened out. Then he took a deep breath and plunged in. "I, um, wanted to ask you something."

"Sure."

"I'm going to a sweet sixteen party on Saturday. It's kind of dorky, I know, but I thought I'd see if you wanted to go with me." The last few words came out in a rush, and Jordan gave himself a mental slap for acting like such a wimp.

The color drained from Rachel's face. "You're asking me for a date?"

"No," Jordan said quickly. "Not a date. I mean, you know, not a *date* date."

Rachel giggled, her cheeks dimpling.

"It would just be you and me going to a party with my mom, my dad, my four brothers, their dates, my aunt Carla, her three ex-husbands, a couple of hundred guests, and . . . oh yeah, my cousin Margaret, whose birthday it is."

"No partridge in a pear tree?" Rachel asked, her eyes sparkling.

Jordan laughed. "There may be one. You never know with the Sullivans."

"You're right. It's not a date. It's a circus."

Jordan laughed again. "Yeah. I just thought it might be fun to go together."

Rachel's face flushed red, but she met his gaze without looking away. "Thank you. That sounds fun. I'd love to go."

Then she turned and almost ran into the school building.

"See?" Jordan said to himself. "Maybe she ran away, but not until after she said yes. That wasn't so hard."

Twelve

"Someday you'll look back on this and laugh," Sky muttered, smearing concealer underneath her eyes. She'd locked herself in a stall and cried. Now she was standing in front of the mirror, covering up the water damage.

She examined her reflection. Not bad— if you didn't look too closely. And nobody seemed very interested in looking at her at all. They were too busy looking at Rachel Harris.

In the distance she heard the first bell. Fifth period would be starting soon, but she just couldn't face it. It was history period. She'd have to sit in there and listen to everybody ooh and ahh over Rachel Harris, and it would just be more than she could stand.

Two seconds later she hated herself. Did she really begrudge poor little Rachel

Harris her measly five minutes in the spotlight? What kind of a friend was she? She was a miserable worm of a friend.

Get a grip and get to class, she told herself firmly. *And stop being a spoiled brat who can't stand it just because somebody else gets a little attention.*

Sky hurried out of the ladies' room and into the school building. The halls were empty. Classes had started.

She stopped by her locker and then hurried toward Ms. Farley's room, pausing outside the door. Maybe if Sky worked it right, she could slip in when Ms. Farley turned to write on the board.

"Okay," she heard the teacher say. "Has anybody come up with a project? Rachel?"

Sky peeked around the corner and saw Rachel with her hand raised.

Rachel stood. "I thought a time capsule might be a good idea. We could take stuff that's meaningful, that says something about us and the world we live in, and seal it up. In a hundred years people in the future can open it and see what we were like."

There was a burst of whispers and a few whistles from around the room.

"What made you think of that?" Ms. Farley asked.

Rachel shrugged. "I don't know. I was just trying to come up with something creative and . . . that's what I came up with."

Sky felt dizzy. Rachel wasn't giving Sky any credit at all. Rachel had even used Sky's exact words to explain the project.

Unfortunately Ms. Farley spotted her at that moment. "Sky? What are you doing out there? Class has started."

Sky walked into the room. Her eyes met Rachel's. Rachel dropped her gaze for a split second, then stared Sky right in the eye, lifting her chin defiantly.

Sky swayed slightly, feeling like she'd been hit on the back of the head.

"Sky," Ms. Farley said sharply. "Is something wrong?"

"I . . . I don't feel well," Sky managed to say through her tight throat.

Ms. Farley's face softened. "Why don't you go to the nurse's office?" she said kindly. "Your partner seems to have the project well in hand. She can catch you up on it later."

Sky backed out of the room, tears blinding her eyes. This was a nightmare. She could hardly even believe it. After all she had done for Rachel—giving her her own identity—she'd stolen Sky's, anyway.

Rachel Harris and Sky Foley had exchanged lives.

Rachel was pretty and popular.

And Sky felt like an ugly, worthless loser hiding out in the nurse's office.

She'd tell the nurse that she was having a relapse of her morning stomach crud and ask her to call Sky's dad.

It was no lie now. Sky did feel sick. Heartsick.

Thirteen

"Feeling any better?" Sky's mother put down a tray with a pot of herbal tea and salted crackers and felt Sky's forehead. "No fever; that's good," she murmured.

"I'm okay," Sky said, sitting up in bed.

Her mother poured out a steaming mug and handed it to her. "Carrie and Alex are here. Feel like seeing them?"

Sky blinked. Carrie and Alex were here? Was it possible they hadn't completely forgotten she was their best friend? "Sure," she said. "Why not?"

Mrs. Foley raised her brows. "Why not? That doesn't sound very enthusiastic."

Sky didn't feel like going into the whole sorry day with her mom, so she just smiled. "I guess I'm not feeling all that social."

"I'll tell them you're asleep," Mrs. Foley said.

"No!" Sky cried. Maybe they had come

over to apologize. Maybe they had realized how incredibly insensitive they had been to her at lunch.

If so, Sky was prepared to forgive them. She was a big person. Way bigger than Rachel Harris could ever be. "I do want them to come down," she told her mother.

Mrs. Foley looked uncertain. "All right," she said after a few moments. "But if you start to feel nauseous, you tell them to come get me. Okay?"

"Sure, Mom," Sky promised. Even though Sky's stomachache was a complete fake, if her friends gushed enough about Rachel, she probably *would* get nauseous.

A few moments later Carrie and Alex came in, smiling as if they had no clue at all that Sky's feelings were majorly bruised.

Alex adjusted the bill of her Supersonics cap. "Feeling any better?"

"You sure look better," Carrie said. "When you came into history class, you looked like the undead."

"Something made me feel seriously sick," Sky said softly.

"Something you ate?" Alex asked.

Sky shook her head. "Something I

heard." Sky tried to fight it, but tears came spilling out of her eyes.

"Sky! What's wrong?" Alex asked. "What is it?"

"Rachel," Sky managed to choke out. "You were right, Carrie. You were right and I was wrong and I am so dumb."

Carrie pulled a tissue from the box by Sky's bed and handed it to her. "No, you're not," she said in a voice that for Carrie was soft.

"What did Rachel do?" Alex asked.

"She stole my idea," Sky choked. "The time capsule thing. It was my idea. But she acted like it was all hers."

"Are you serious?" Alex asked.

"That was *your* idea?" Carrie demanded.

"From the beginning." Sky managed a slight smile. "My dad's car inspired me."

"I believe that," Alex said.

"What a total psychopath!" Carrie exclaimed angrily. "She talked about that project for about fifteen minutes and never even mentioned you. I *thought* it was weird. It sounded like such a Sky idea."

"I feel like the stupidest person in the world," Sky moaned.

"It's not your fault," Alex said. "I mean, how could you know?"

"Yeah," Carrie agreed. "She totally weaseled her way into your life. But don't feel dumb. We were all fooled. Jordan even asked her to go to a sweet sixteen party with him."

Sky dropped the cup of tea on the floor. "What?"

Alex grabbed some napkins and started blotting up the tea.

"And get this," Carrie added. "He did it because *I* told everybody to be nice to Rachel for your sake. So if anybody's dumb, it's me."

Carrie stood and began to pace as best she could in the small space. "Okay. What are we going to do about this?"

"Do?" Sky repeated.

"Yeah. We've got to do something. We can't let her get away with this. Rachel needs to learn that Sky made Rachel. And she can break her just as easily," Carrie said.

"How?" Alex asked.

"We do it like this." Carrie walked up to Alex, pretending she was walking up to Rachel. "Rachel! Great outfit. Did you swipe it from Sky's closet?"

104

Alex laughed nervously. "Kind of Amy, but I like it."

Sky shook her head. "*Too* Amy. Let's just forget it. It's not all that important."

"She deserves to be emotionally nuked," Carrie insisted. "We've got to draw a line in the sand. You can't just do nothing. I mean, that would make you as spineless as Rachel, pre-remodel, that is."

"Makeover," Alex and Sky corrected.

"Whatever," Carrie grunted.

Sky chewed a nail. What Rachel had done was rotten with a capital *R*. She'd pretended to be a shy Sky Foley fan when she was really a scheming manipulator, determined to steal Sky's life out from under her.

Sky threw back the covers and stood. Where was it written that nice people just had to take it and not fight back? Rachel had skunked Sky. Now it was Sky's turn to skunk Rachel.

"Okay," she said. "We'll do it. Bombard her with backhanded compliments all day until she crumbles."

"Do we tell the guys?" Carrie asked. "Get them in on it?"

Alex shook her head. "No. You know how Sam is. No matter how heinous somebody is, he doesn't want to get involved. And Jordan's still got to go to that party with her."

"Yeah. But he only asked her because he thought it would make Sky happy," Carrie argued. "He can just tell Rachel the deal's off—can't he?"

Alex shook her head. "Not if he wants to keep a good guy image. At least that's what my brother says. Once a guy asks a girl to do something, he's got to follow through unless she cancels or dies."

"Let's not make Jordan choose between being a good guy and being my friend," Sky said. "Let's keep this our secret."

"Okay, then," Carrie agreed. "It's just us. But tomorrow when the lunch bell rings, we go into action. By fifth period, if Project Payback has been a success, Rachel Harris will probably be in Principal Cashen's office, begging to change schools."

Sky swallowed. That sounded a little harsh. "You guys—"

"By the way," Carrie interrupted, "your hair looks totally cool."

"Ditto," Alex confirmed.

"You really think so?" Sky squealed.

"Supermodel all the way," Alex said, popping her gum.

Sky pushed her concerns about Project Payback aside and grinned. Someone had finally noticed her.

The Final Showdown

"Jordan?"

"Yes, Mom?"

"It's almost dusk."

"I know, Mom."

"Do you have anything to tell me?"

"Rachel Harris."

"Rachel Harris? Who's Rachel Harris?"

"A girl I know. I asked her to the party."

A wide smile spread across Mrs. Sullivan's face. "Is she cute?"

"She's a babe," Jordan confirmed.

Mrs. Sullivan picked up the phone. "I'll call Margaret's mother right now." While Mrs. Sullivan dialed, Jordan skittered out of the living room and ran upstairs, breathing heavily—like a man who had dodged not one but four bullets that day.

He'd actually finessed it so that everybody was happy. His mom. Carrie. Alex. And happiest of all—Sky.

Fourteen

"So everybody is happy. After Saturday the whole thing will be over and done with, and we can all get on with our lives." Jordan still couldn't quite believe his luck.

Jordan followed Sam through the crowded hallway to the water fountain. Sam bent over and took a drink. "Are you looking forward to it?" he asked Jordan between sips. "The party, I mean?"

Sam stepped aside, and Jordan took a long drink, then stood and wiped his mouth with the back of his hand. "You know what? I am. Now that I don't have to worry about who's going to be mad at me, I can actually relax and enjoy the ride. My dad picked up the tux at the cleaners, and I tried it on."

"Yeah? It looks good?"

"It looks great." Jordan blushed when he heard himself. He sounded like a girl or something. "I just mean I don't look like a total dork," he amended.

Sam grinned. "Tuxes and big parties are totally cool. I mean, if it's good enough for the Bondster . . ."

"Have you ever had to wear one?" Jordan asked.

Sam nodded. "I was an usher at my uncle's wedding last year. It was fun. I danced and everything."

"Ugh! Dancing. I hope Rachel can dance."

"Can you dance?" Sam asked.

"No. That's why I was hoping Rachel could."

Sam laughed. "Here she comes. You can ask her."

Jordan looked up and saw Rachel weaving her way through the crowd in their direction. Jordan still couldn't quite believe it was actually Rachel Harris. She looked really *pretty*.

As Rachel got closer Jordan noticed that her eyes looked sort of red and watery.

"Jordan," she said. "I need to talk to you."

Sam cleared his throat. "I gotta get to class, anyway. See ya."

Great, Sam, Jordan thought, staring at his friend's retreating back. *Bail on me just when it sounds like things are about to get serious.*

Jordan turned to Rachel and frowned. He had a bad feeling about this. "What's up?"

Rachel chewed on her lower lip for a few seconds before responding. "Listen, I can't go to the party with you."

Jordan's stomach flopped. Images of his crazed mother with a meat cleaver flew through his mind. "What? What do you mean?"

"I can't go," she repeated.

"Why can't you go?" he asked, his voice breaking. "I know. It's your mom. She doesn't know me. Am I right? If that's the problem, no problem. I'll come over and meet her."

Rachel shook her head sorrowfully. "No. That's not it."

Jordan began to perspire. If Rachel backed out, he'd be back at square one. Only he'd be dead, too. "I'll have my mom call her and run it all down with her. Your mom probably wants to be sure there are going to be chaperons and all that. Don't worry."

"That's not it," Rachel said, practically shouting. "I just can't go because I . . . I don't *want* to go."

Jordan felt as if he had been slapped. Was Rachel telling him she was too good to go to a party with him? That she was too cool and popular now?

"Well, okay, then," Jordan said softly. "Whatever." He turned and began to walk away.

Rachel ran after him. "I don't mean I don't want to go because I don't want to go with *you*. I mean I don't want to go because it wouldn't be right."

Jordan stopped. The girl was obviously crazy. "What are you talking about?"

Rachel backed away, her cheeks reddening. "I can't explain. I just can't. It's just too complicated."

"My mom's already told the hostess you're coming. She gave her your name so she could put it on a place card—whatever that means."

Rachel let out a little moan.

"Rachel, I need you to come with me. I have to bring somebody, and I—" Jordan broke off. This was unbelievable. He,

Jordan Sullivan, was actually standing in the hall of Robert Lowell Middle School *begging* the school nerd to go to a party with him. "Never mind," he said harshly. "Just forget it."

"Believe me," Rachel said, "you don't want to go to a party with me. I'm a horrible person. Probably the most horrible person you ever met."

Jordan really began to wonder if Rachel was some kind of head case.

Rachel took a step back. It was weird, but she looked like plain Rachel Harris again. Meek and apologetic. "I just can't go," she said in a faint voice. "You should ask . . . somebody else." With that, Rachel turned away, disappearing into the crowded hallway.

Jordan groaned and leaned back against the wall.

"I wonder how much a ticket to Africa actually costs," he muttered.

Project Payback

11:10 A.M. Rachel Harris sneaks into the art room. There's no art class during third period, so she has it all to herself.

11:15 A.M. Sky drums her nails on her desk and tries to ignore the sickish feeling in her stomach. Being mean—even to Rachel—feels bad. But only doormats don't fight back.

11:20 A.M. Rachel finds the jewelry-making tools, selects a clasp, and goes to work on the bracelet she's making for Sky.

11:25 A.M. Carrie watches the clock. So far, so good. All systems are go. She checks her list of "completely evil and devastating things to say to Rachel." It's quite long. It'll be hard to choose, but at least it was agreed that Carrie would get first shot.

11:30 A.M. Rachel carefully attaches the clasp to the woven leather-and-bead braid she made out of her only headband. It's not nearly nice enough for Sky, but the headband was the nicest thing Rachel owned—not including the clothes Sky made for her.

11:35 A.M. Alex wonders how many other totally evil people are walking around the planet cleverly disguised as harmless nerds.

11:40 A.M. Rachel goofs up the clasp. If it was for her, she'd just leave it and wear it that way. But since it's an apology for Sky, it's got to be perfect. Rachel clips off the clasp and starts over.

11:45 A.M. Jordan wonders if Rachel backing out is a girl thing and if Carrie, Alex, or Sky might be able to shed some light on the situation.

11:50 A.M. Sky takes some deep breaths. Ten more minutes and it's "show time."

11:55 A.M. Carrie's foot begins to bounce. She wishes the bell would ring already.

11:57 A.M. Rachel finishes the clasp, runs to put away the tools, and hastily writes *I'm sorry* on a slip of paper. If she hurries, she can catch Sky coming out of class.

12:00 NOON The bell rings.

12:01 P.M. Carrie hits the hall, her eyes scanning back and forth in search of Rachel.

12:02 P.M. Alex hits the hall, preparing to stand tall with her buddies.

12:02 P.M. Sky hits the hall, her stomach churning.

12:03:05 P.M. Rachel spots Sky and starts in her direction.

12:03:05 P.M. Alex sees Rachel, catches Carrie's eye, and points toward Rachel.

12:03:10 P.M. Carrie locks onto target and starts closing in.

116

12:03:15 P.M. Rachel, having no idea that Torpedo Carrie is zooming in, calls out Sky's name.

12:03:20 P.M. Scene unfolds in front of Alex as if in slow motion. Carrie is five feet from Rachel. Rachel is three feet from Sky. Carrie opens mouth, preparing to deliver.

12:03:22 P.M. Rachel holds something out to Sky. Alex can't hear what Rachel is saying, but she can see her lips forming the words, "I'm sorry."

12:03:25 P.M. Sky jumps between Carrie and Rachel. Carrie careens off course, exploding harmlessly against Mel Eng. Mel Eng gives Carrie a dirty look, but Carrie is otherwise undamaged.

12:03:30 P.M. Sky and Rachel duck into an empty classroom and close the door. The clock stops. Project Payback is canceled until further notice.

Fifteen

Sky closed the door, looked through the little glass window, and signaled Alex and Carrie to go on to lunch.

Carrie scowled, raising her brows and holding out her hands.

Alex said something to her and tugged at Carrie's long, drapey black sleeve. Carrie shrugged, and they walked off in the direction of the cafeteria. Turning away from the door, Sky examined the bracelet that Rachel had thrust into her hands.

There was a long, long silence. "This is pretty," Sky said in a flat tone.

"It's for you," Rachel said. "I made it."

"Why?"

Rachel hung her head and fidgeted with her fingernails. Sky noticed that they weren't painted today.

"I wanted to say I'm sorry, and I didn't know how."

Sky sat down at a desk. She had no clue what to say, so she didn't say anything.

Sky swallowed, feeling close to tears. Up until now, all she had felt was anger. She hadn't realized how hurt her feelings had been.

"Why did you do it?" Sky asked.

"Because I wanted to be the center of attention," Rachel blurted out. "I'd never had any friends. Nobody had ever paid any attention to me. Once the attention started, I was so afraid it would stop, I wanted to do anything to keep it going. So I acted like your idea was mine. It was a horrible thing to do."

Sky reached into her tote and pulled out a tissue. She could feel her throat tightening. "The horrible thing you did was pretend to be my friend when you weren't," Sky said, choking.

Rachel didn't say anything. She looked at Sky with a face that was pale and ashamed.

"But . . . but . . . I can't really blame you for that," Sky went on. "Because, well, I guess I sort of did the same thing to you."

A look of pain creased Rachel's face, but

then she lifted her chin slightly. "I knew it," she said in a firm voice. "I knew you didn't really want to be my friend. You just felt sorry for me."

Sky felt worse than she had ever felt in her whole life. "The horrible one here is me. Not you."

Rachel blinked. "What are you talking about?"

"I'm a horrible person," Sky admitted. "I didn't do all those things for you because I'm nice. I did them because . . . well . . . I thought if I acted like your friend, you would let me be in charge of the whole history project." Sky chuckled wryly. "So I guess what you did served me right."

"You didn't have to be nice to me to get what you wanted," Rachel said. "I was the kind of person who would never have argued with anybody more popular than me—which means the entire population of the civilized world."

Sky smiled. "Did you notice that you said *was*, not am?"

Rachel thought about it a minute. "You're right. It was a slip. I *am* the kind of person who would never argue with anybody more popular than me."

"Would you stop with the I'm-a-lowly-*E.-coli*-bacterium stuff?"

"I'll give it up at New Year's."

"No. Give it up now," Sky said. "You've got a lot going for you, Rachel."

"But if I'm not Rachel Harris, champion girl dork, and I'm not Rachel Harris, Sky Foley wanna-be, who am I?"

"That's what you have to find out." Sky smiled and turned the bracelet on her arm. "But you've got a great sense of humor and a great sense of style, and you *are* a nice person—you wouldn't have made this for me if you weren't."

"Nice people don't act so rotten. They don't have to make bracelets to make up for how rotten they've been."

"Everybody acts rotten sometimes— even me," Sky said. "I was plotting to get you back."

"You were?" Rachel seemed almost pleased to hear it.

"Yeah. I was. I'm gonna have to remember to call off my attack dogs," Sky said.

"Carrie and Alex?" Rachel asked.

"Yep," Sky said, smiling.

"Scary." Rachel gave a comical little shudder.

Sky took a deep breath and looked Rachel in the eyes. "I'd still like to be friends. For real. So here's the deal: I'll accept your apology if you'll accept mine."

"No."

"No?"

"No," Rachel repeated. "I don't want an apology. I'd really like a favor."

"What kind of a favor?" Sky asked curiously. Did Rachel want Sky's help with another outfit?

"Explain to Jordan that I really like him and I think he's a great guy, but the reason I can't go to a big party with him is I'm not up to the social strain. I don't think I've quite made it to 'party girl' status yet," she joked.

Sky choked on a laugh.

"Tell him to call me when Margaret gets married," Rachel added.

Sky laughed again. Pretty soon the two girls were talking and chatting and laughing. Before they knew it, the bell rang, lunch was over, and it was time for fifth period.

Sky and Rachel walked out of the classroom and turned toward history class.

"We're gonna have to get to work on our history project this afternoon," Rachel said.

"Yeah. I think we're officially behind now," Sky added, opening the door to the classroom.

"It's okay. Ms. Farley's giving us the class period to work on it today," Rachel said.

"Sweet. Let's snag the big table in the back of the room," Sky said, heading past the desks.

"I'll be right there," Rachel called after her. "After I tell Ms. Farley all about *your* project idea."

"It's *our* project," Sky said with a smile. "It doesn't matter whose idea it was in the beginning."

"It matters to me," Rachel said, tossing her hair back over her shoulders. She squared her shoulders and walked toward the big gray desk at the front of the room.

Sky shrugged but grinned. This was definitely the beginning of a great friendship.

Sixteen

Carrie pulled her covers up to her chin and glared at the ceiling. It was torture not knowing what had happened. Rachel and Sky had looked very chummy in history class. Then Sky hadn't been on the bus, so Carrie had called Sky this afternoon, but Mrs. Foley had told her Sky was out. Then Sky's line had been busy all night.

Carrie made a mental note not to make any more friends who didn't have call waiting.

Just as she closed her eyes, the phone rang. Carrie threw back the covers, ran to the extension on her desk, and picked it up. "Hello?"

"Project Payback is officially canceled," Sky said.

"Where have you been?" Carrie demanded.

"Rachel and I spent most of the

afternoon at her house. Her mom had an old trunk in the attic that she said we could use as the time capsule. We cleaned off all the rust and stuff. So start picking out your very best short story."

Carrie shook her head and wondered if she was getting a lot of waxy buildup in her ear. "Did I hear you correctly? You spent the day with Rachel? Horrible Rachel Harris?"

Sky giggled. "Yeah. And she's not so horrible after all. In fact, I like her."

"You would," Carrie said dryly.

"You would, too," Sky insisted. Then she told Carrie about the bracelet and how Rachel had apologized for trying to be Sky. "She's sorry about what she did to me," Sky said finally. "So let's just forget about it and move on. Okay?"

"What about what she did to Jordan?" Carrie said.

"Well," Sky said. "I understand why she doesn't want to go. And tomorrow I'll explain it to Jordan."

Sky's voice sounded a little tight. Carrie knew that was the signal to drop it. "Okay," Carrie said. "Whatever you say.

I'm just glad everything's cool with you. See you tomorrow."

"See you," Sky said, clicking off.

Carrie got back in her bed and pulled up the covers. After twisting herself up in her sheets for twenty minutes, she threw them back again. The whole thing was just too weird. She couldn't sleep without talking to somebody about it.

Seventeen

Sam closed his skateboarding magazine and turned off the light. A split second later, the phone rang. Sam wondered if there was some electrical connection between his bedside lamp and the phone. It seemed like it always rang the minute he decided to go to sleep.

Fortunately the phone was by his bed. "Hello?"

"Are you asleep?" Carrie asked.

"Not yet. What's up?"

Within two minutes he was sorry he asked.

When Carrie got to the part about Rachel stealing Sky's idea, he decided he was never going to answer his phone again.

When she got to the part about Project Payback, he considered having the phone taken out of his room.

When she got to the part about Rachel making Sky a bracelet and Sky apologizing, he began to think it was sort of a neat story.

When she got to the part about Rachel not wanting to go to the party with Jordan, he began thinking. He didn't usually get involved in other people's problems, but Jordan was a pal, and he needed help.

Eighteen

Alex heaved a sigh of relief when Matt finally hung up the phone. He'd been talking to his new girlfriend for hours. Alex ran into the kitchen and put her hand on the receiver.

Before she could dial, it rang. "Hello?" she said.

"Were you sitting on the phone?" Sam asked with a laugh. "It didn't even finish the first ring."

Alex smiled. "I was just getting ready to call Carrie."

"Okay. Well, I won't keep you long, but I just talked to Carrie, and here's what she told me about Rachel and Sky."

Sam took a deep breath and started talking.

Alex couldn't help thinking how for a guy who said he didn't like to get involved with people's problems, Sam had a few pretty good ideas.

129

It was almost better than getting the story from Carrie. Carrie tended to go off on tangents, but Sam stuck right to the good parts.

"So Rachel doesn't want to go to the party with Jordan. And you gotta figure that in spite of the happy ending, Sky probably feels like she's taken a couple of blows. So . . . I had this idea about something that might cheer her up. . . ."

Nineteen

Jordan lay on his bed, his eyes wide open, staring at the ceiling. He hadn't had the nerve to tell his mother that he was once again dateless. Forget the date thing. Once again without a girl with whom to dance.

Maybe on the big night he could say Rachel had gotten the measles or something.

He closed his eyes and pictured himself at the party. Just a boy, a tux, a place card, and an empty chair.

Gag. It sounded like the lyrics to a bad country song.

He heard the phone ring out in the hall. Then he heard heavy footsteps go to answer it. He heard the low rumble of a postpuberty male voice. Then the heavy footsteps moved in the direction of his room.

The door opened. Jordan half expected to hear, "Fee, fie, fo, fum."

Instead his oldest brother turned on the overhead light, blinding him. "Telephone for you, fart face. It's a . . . giiirrrllllll," he informed Jordan in a silly falsetto.

Jordan got up and stumbled out of his room toward the phone on the hall table. "Hello?"

"Jordan. It's me. Alex."

"Hey. What's up?"

"I just talked to Sam. We hate to tell you what to do, but if you don't ask Sky to go to the sweet sixteen party with you, Carrie, Sam, and I will never speak to you again."

Jordan felt a silly grin spread across his face. "Really?"

"Really. Sky's had a major emotional roller-coaster ride. And you know how girly she is. A sweet sixteen party complete with corsage would probably be a big thrill," Alex said matter-of-factly.

Jordan could barely contain his joy. "Well, if you think so . . ."

"Absolutely," Alex said. "We insist."

"Well, if you insist, then I guess I'll ask her."

Jordan hung up the phone, waited two seconds, then jumped into the air. *"Yes!"* he shouted happily.

He couldn't believe it. Saved again. Alex and Carrie were actually *insisting* that he invite Sky. They were happy. He was happy. His mother would be happy—once she got over the shock of Sky not being somebody named Rachel Harris.

Twenty

Jordan planted his feet on the parquet dance floor and twirled Sky under his arm. The hem of her black velvet dress fluttered out as she circled like a ballerina.

Nearby, Mr. and Mrs. Sullivan danced along to the music of the Seattle Samba Kings.

"You two are great dancers," Mr. Sullivan said with a smile. "Where did you learn?"

"I didn't," Jordan answered. "I think it's the tux. It seems to know what to do, so I'm just letting it lead."

Sky grinned. "You look great, Jor-*dumb*."

"So do you," Jordan said happily. She really did. Even Aunt Carla, who had piles of cash from her many divorces and always wore the latest fashions, told Sky she looked adorable.

She'd complimented Jordan on his tux, too.

And the ex-husband with the Mercedes dealership had told Jordan to come see him if he wanted a summer job. It paid to dress for success.

The music stopped, and the guests applauded. It was a big party. So big, Jordan hadn't even seen his four brothers in the last hour, which made a great party *beyond* great.

"Let's check out the dessert table," Jordan suggested.

"Sounds like a plan." Sky and Jordan wove through the crowd until they found the dessert buffet.

"Wow!" Sky whistled. "Forget the dinner. Forget the dancing. Forget this gorgeous club. *This* is the main event."

"Let's have one of everything," Jordan suggested. He handed Sky a plate and took one for himself. They worked their way down the table, snagging a lemon square, a chocolate truffle mousse with raspberry sauce, a miniature pecan pie, an almond tart, and last but not least a fruit cup.

They went back to their table and settled down to pig out.

"Where do we start?" Jordan asked.

"The lemon tart," Sky answered. "Then

we'll work our way through the chocolate stuff. We'll save the fruit for last."

"You know, when Mom told me about this thing, I thought it was going to be horrible. But I'm having fun. Thanks for coming with me."

"Thanks for asking me," Sky said with a smile. "You're not too disappointed about Rachel, are you?"

He shook his head. "No. That would have been a strain. Too much like a date— you know—because we don't know each other."

Sky took a bite of the lemon square. "Wow," she marveled. "The perfect mix of sweet and sour."

Jordan licked his lips. "Sort of like life."

"Sort of like people," Sky added.

"Sort of like us," they said in unison.